TIESHA IN TH

MW00965695

By K.D. Patrick

Illustrations by Hugh Rookwood

And Surge Chana

Book Design by Michelle Sison

All the Best!

Surge

KOOL PRESS
Toronto New York London Auckland Sydney
St George New Mexico

Tiesha in the land of Faraway is a work of fiction. Names, places, and incidents either are a product of the author's imagination or are used fictitiously.

ISBN 0-9734152-0-7

Visit Kool Press on the World Wide Web at

http://www.koolpress.com

Dedicated in loving memory of my grandmother, Sylvesta Patrick, who taught me to love reading and storytelling and who listened patiently to all my stories from early childhood through adolescence to grown man. Your encouragement and advice shaped and molded my talent. I feel your presence as you continue to walk with me. For my children, Tiesha and Kyrel, who are my inspirations and most precious gifts, and for my heart, Tamara. For my mother, Margaret, my hero and role model. You are love and wisdom personified. For my father, Godfrey. For my sisters and brother, Jewel, Donna and Corey, my nieces and nephews, Janelle and Emma, Jeremy and Dylan and for all my family, my clan. You enrich my life. For Patrick Thomas, my brother of the mind and spirit. And of course for my friend and editor Claudette. May you all travel your life's journey carrying love in your hearts and a song in your souls.

-CHAPTER ONE-

A Historic Meeting

Tiesha awoke to the sound of raindrops pattering on the roof. For a moment she remained snuggled beneath the warm blankets feeling cozy. Then she remembered what day it was.

"Oh no," She cried, jumping out of bed and hurrying over to the window. Pressing her face up against the windowpane, she gazed out, past the raindrops splattering against the glass. At the sight of the dark overcast sky and the pouring rain, she sighed in disappointment.

"It's Saturday, no school and I was looking forward to start building my tree house with daddy today," she moaned dismally.

"Oh well, I guess I will just have to find ways of amusing myself indoors," she told herself. "Hmmm!" Maybe I can help mommy bake coconut bread, she mused, trying to think up things that she would enjoy doing indoors on a rainy day.

After breakfast Tiesha went back upstairs to her room where she wrote a letter to her friend Shannon, who was away in Vancouver. Putting her pen away after finishing the letter, Tiesha spied her favorite book lying on the old trunk her grandmother had given her when she was four years old. A smile lit up her face, she had already read the book many times but she never got tired of reading it over. The book was a collection of stories all set in a magical world called the Land of Faraway.

That's what I will do, I'll read the Book of Faraway, she decided. "Now which story should I read first?"

Soon she was sitting with the book opened, enjoying the first story in the book. It was about a little sprite name Neeka, who got lost while attending a fair in Fief, the land of the Elfin-faer.

Tiesha had only just finished the story when suddenly, she heard a musical sound, just like the tinkling of bells and a rainbow appeared above the open pages of her book. In a shower of twinkling dust a tiny woman with soft satiny wings appeared. She was beautiful and she wore a dress of purest gossamer.

Tiesha's eyes popped open wide in surprise at the amazing sight.

"Hello, don't be afraid," said the tiny Elfin woman in soft lilting voice that seem to tickle Tiesha's ears.

"You… You are Elfin-faer!" Tiesha exclaimed in a voice of wonder.

"Yes, I am," said the tiny woman with a deep bow. "I'm Gossamer, the queen of the Elfin-faer people. And I have desperate need of your help my dear."

"Am I… Am I dreaming?" asked Tiesha rubbing at her eyes with the back of her hand.

"No you are not. I'm as real as real can be," smiled the Elfin-faer queen. "And so is the Land of Faraway."

Just then the legs of Elfin-faer queen began to fade. "Oh dear!" she exclaimed. "My magic is almost gone. If you are to come with me to the Land of Faraway to help us, we must go before my magic fades away completely."

"Maybe a grown up can help you. I'm only eight years old you see and I'm not at all sure how I can help." Tiesha said with a warm smile. She still felt as if she were dreaming but was trying her best to believe what was happening.

"Sadly, grown-ups cannot come to the land of Faraway," explained Gossamer, the queen, "Only very special children. I wish I could explain everything right now but I can't, there isn't enough time. Please you must help us or all hope is lost!"

The tiny queen not only sounded sincere but she seemed very familiar as well. Tiesha felt as if she had met her before and somehow she knew the Elfin-faer queen meant her no harm. So after a moment of thought Tiesha smiled brightly and said. "Ok."

"Yes," she said with firm resolve. "Of course I will help you."

"Thank you my dear," said the Elfin-faer queen. "Now get ready, off to the Land of Faraway we go!"

And with a wave of a dainty little hand, twinkling dust which smelled like spring flowers, filled the air and Tiesha felt the real world fade away as she was transported on a rainbow to the Land of Faraway.

CHAPTER TWO

A Faraway Land and a Unicorn

It was the most marvelous thing, one moment Tiesha was in her room and in the next she found herself somewhere else. She was high in a very clear blue sky, flying through the air. She giggled in delight as she soared through a large shimmering rainbow.

Tiesha loved flying; she flew on planes whenever she went to visit her grandmother who lived in Barbados, a beautiful small island in the Caribbean. Though flying in a plane was fun and exciting; the kind of flying she was doing now, was even better. She could feel the wind on her face as it blew her hair out behind her.

"I'm flying. I'm really flying," she cried out happily, turning her head to look at the Elfin-faer queen flying along beside her. "I'm flying like a bird."

"Yes, it's Elfin-faer magic," said the Elfin-faer queen proudly. "Welcome to the land of Faraway and Fief, the kingdom of the Elfin-faer."

Tiesha looked down, stretched out below her was a land of rollicking hills and beautiful green meadows dotted with wild flowers of every size and color she could have imagined. Upon the land stood the most wonderful houses she had ever seen. The houses were dainty and looked just like the ones in her fairy tale books, with graceful spires and quaint chimneys. The roofs and walls of each house were covered in flowers. The air smelled of fresh flowers and sweet spices.

At the center of all the houses stood the grand mystical palace and it was a wonder to see. It twinkled with all the colors of the rainbow and gave Tiesha a warm glowing feeling inside her tummy.

Together Tiesha and the Elfin-faer queen sailed downward

to land in the palace's courtyard, beside a garden full of beautiful rainbow roses. The scent of the roses immediately reminded Tiesha of a candy factory she had visited on a field trip with her school classmates. The factory smelled of an assortment of candy that was being made there.

"It's beautiful," breathed Tiesha. "Just like my grandmother's garden of tropical flowers."

"Yes, but this beauty will soon be gone. Ugliness will replace it, all because of Grom, the Goblin King," said the Elfin-faer queen sadly. "He is the one responsible for my dying magic."

"How is he able to do that?" asked Tiesha feeling alarmed at the thought of someone ruining all the beauty around her and destroying the very magic that had brought her to this land of wonders and that had allowed her to fly.

In a sad voice the queen began explaining how the evil Goblin King was destroying the flower magic with his great malevolent machines. Tiesha was dismayed to learn that the king's goblin subjects traveled the lands of Faraway, using their terrible machines to gobble up all the trees and flowers. The machines were big and noisy, clanking and rumbling along on giant wheels, the engines burning the flowers and trees for fuel.

As the engines burned the trees and flowers, they produced great clouds of black smoke, which choked the skies of Faraway, seeping into the clouds, causing acidic rains that burned the skin of the Elfin-faer people when it fell. The machines' engines also leaked thick oily liquids that soaked into the ground poisoning the lands, turning the once fertile soil barren. This blight caused such long-term damage that neither flowers, plants or trees would ever grow on that land again.

"How horrible!" cried Tiesha, she could not help but feel a little bit afraid of the Goblin King, picturing him as a mean gruesome brute. And while she did not like to think bad thoughts of anyone, the Goblin King certainly did not sound like a very nice person.

"Yes," agreed the Elfin-faer queen. "Flower magic is very precious, and with so few flowers left, there isn't enough pollen dust to make Faer magic. Soon the Goblin King's machines will reach the kingdom of Fief and then all will be lost."

"But how can I help?" asked Tiesha doubtfully. "What can one little girl possibly do to stop the Goblin King if your magic cannot stop him?"

"Well one special little girl can do what all the Elfin-faer people cannot. You can take a message across The Twisted Lands to the great Dragon King to the north," said the queen.

"Why can't you take the message to the Dragon King yourself?" asked Tiesha looking as puzzled as she felt.

The Elfin-faer queen quickly explained that the north, where the Dragon King resided, was bitterly cold. It was always winter there, and the Elfin-faer could not survive in cold temperatures without magical spells to protect them from the cold.

"It's always summer here in the kingdom of Fief you see." She said gesturing to the panoramic beauty around them.

Tiesha was amazed. "Really?"

"Yes," said the Elfin-faer queen. "But you, Tiesha, are from a land that has both summer and winter. So you are much better suited to make this journey than we. That's why we need your help; besides, you are special in other ways which you will one day discover."

"What do you mean?" asked Tiesha curiously.

"That will be revealed in the proper time, there is a season for all things under the sun," smiled the Elfin-faer queen her eyes twinkling.

Tiesha smiled because she knew the tiny queen would explain no further, so it would do no good to press the matter. Grown-ups always seem to say things like that whenever they intend to avert further discussion.

Instead she said after a moments thought. "Surely you could use your magic to protect you from the cold of the Dragon King's kingdom."

"Ordinarily, yes, but our magic is dying and very strong spells are needed to protect us from the cold of the Northern lands. We don't have enough Faer magic left to keep us warm on such a lengthy and cold journey. Besides, the Goblin King has many allies in The Twisted lands. The trolls and the harpies, to name but a few, are helping him to bar our passage through the Twisted-lands to the Dragon King's kingdom beyond." said the queen sadly. "We tried to make the journey before our magic began faltering but every time we were forced back by Grom's allies."

"If these trolls and the others will not let you pass, then surely they're not going to let me pass either." Tiesha said knowingly.

"You are human and it has been a very long time indeed since any humans have been to Faraway so your appearance should confuse Grom's allies. They will not realize right away that you are our messenger, so this will increase the chance of you slipping by them. And we have arranged for allies of our own to help you along the way," explained the Elfin-faer queen. "Ah, here's one of them now."

"Hello," said a high musical voice in Tiesha's ear, giving her quite a start.

Tiesha turned around and saw that the voice belonged to a huge silver unicorn with great big wings tucked in to his sides. Tiesha stared in wide-eyed wonder before remembering that it was not polite to stare. Fortunately, the Elfin-faer queen saved her from any further embarrassment by making the appropriate introductions.

"Tiesha meet our good friend Talon the unicorn," the queen said graciously. "Talon, this is Tiesha, our human friend who has so generously agreed to help us in our time of need by undertaking this quest."

"Hello," said Tiesha shyly. "Pleased to meet you."

"And I am especially pleased to make your acquaintance," said the unicorn in his high musical voice. "But time is running out, we must be on our journey for I have just received word that the Goblin King has destroyed yet another forest to the south and is only three days away from reaching the hills of Fief. Climb onto my back dear girl and let us fly."

"Wait," laughed the Elfin-faer queen. "I know you are anxious to begin your journey but Tiesha must be provided some provision, such as refreshments and warm clothing, for this long journey."

"Quite right you are," Talon chuckled. "Whatever was I thinking?"

All it took was a wave of the Elfin-faer queen's hand and the appearance of twinkling dust in the air about Tiesha's small carry bag and it was done. Tiesha felt the bag grow just a little heavier and guessed what had just happened even before the queen's next words.

"There, I have filled your bag with some sandwiches, fruit and cake. There is also a warm Tweedle-silk coat tucked in as well," said the queen. "It has all been magically packed so there's plenty of space left in your bag for any souvenirs you want to collect on your journey."

"Thank you," said Tiesha with a bright smile. She was beginning to understand just how important magic was to the people of Faraway. Even something as simple as packing a bag was done magically.

"You are welcome," smiled the queen floating into the air to wrap her tiny arms around Tiesha in a big hug.

"Hop on little one and we'll be on our way," said the unicorn bending both his forelegs, lowering himself to his knees beside Tiesha.

After a moment's hesitation, Tiesha vaulted up onto Talon's back. Settling astride the unicorn's back she tucked her legs out of the way behind his wings, clutching his thick curly mane with one hand. She was surprised to discover that the unicorn's mane felt softer than her favorite velvet scarf.

"Are you comfortable?" inquired the unicorn once she was in place.

"Yes," answered Tiesha. Except for the wings, being on the unicorn felt just like being on a regular horse, she decided.

Standing and spreading his wings to their full span, Talon said to the Elfin-faer queen. "Fear not, we will reach the Dragon King in time to stop Grom."

"Yes we will. I promise," Tiesha added. "Bye Queen Gossamer."

"Bye. Have a safe journey," called Gossamer, waving to them as the silver unicorn took to the skies with a great leap.

CHAPTER THREE

The Quest Begins

Up, up they flew, until Tiesha thought that he would fly into the sun, but of course he did not. Talon was so happy to be in the skies once again that he could not help but perform a few exuberant aerial stunts.

"Hold tight!" he yelled over his shoulder to Tiesha. And with that he promptly performed a skillful loop the loop. Tiesha squealed in delight as the winged unicorn sailed head over heels through the clouds.

"I didn't know unicorns had wings," said Tiesha. "I knew they could fly but I have never read a book that said they had actual wings."

"Well not all unicorns have wings," laughed Talon. "In fact my people are the rarest of the unicorn family. As for the stories about unicorns you get in your human story books… well I would not be too concerned, for they are highly inaccurate. Many of the tales of magical folk do not portray us exactly as we are but as people imagine or simply want us to be. You'll see as you come to meet more of the magical folk in Faraway."

"I have already discovered that Faraway is even more wonderful than what I had imagined," said Tiesha.

"I do so enjoy the freedom of flying in the wide open skies." Talon announced as he soared up through a fluffy white cloud. Emerging above the cloud he charged forward moving his legs in a cantering run, giving the appearance that he was actually running on the surface of the cloud. "I love clouds." He laughed. "Don't they remind you of cotton candy?"

Looking closely, Tiesha was surprised to discover that the clouds did look a lot like big tuffs of cotton candy. "Why yes, they do remind me of cotton candy. I didn't know you had cotton candy in the Land of Faraway."

"Oh yes," answered Talon. Coming to the end of the cloud he was running on, he leapt off, swooping towards another puff of white looming just ahead of them. "The Wee-Kin make the tastiest cotton candy from spun honey sap of the Bumble flowers that grow in Wee-dale."

"Wee-Kin? Bumble flowers?" said Tiesha wonderingly.

Laughing at the curiosity he could hear in her voice, Talon pulled up in midair and began summoning unicorn magic. His unihorn began to glow and an image of the Wee-Kin, cavorting around in a grassy flower filled dale, surrounded by low rolling hills, appeared in the air before them.

Tiesha breathed a sigh of delight at the sight of the tiny, colorfully dressed people who looked like little flowers with arms and legs. Some were busy turning cartwheels in the grass while others were leaping from the tulip shaped petals of flowers that were striped yellow and black like the body of a bumblebee. She could not resist a chuckle now that she understood how the people and flowers got their names.

"I really like it here. Faraway is a wonderful place with the most interesting inhabitants," Tiesha said, speaking her thoughts aloud. "I wish I could bring all my friends here to enjoy it."

"Hmmm," Talon murmured softly. "It would be nice to have lots of human children to play with again. I remember the sugary treats they would give me in exchange for riding in the sky on my back and for the magical tricks I would perform for them. But that was long ago, before even your grandparents were wee children themselves. You see, Faraway was once part of your world, the human world."

"Really?" Tiesha breathed, immediately wanting to know more. "Is that why we have so many stories about magic?"

"Yes, the memories of the magical folk may be somewhat dim for humans, but your people still remember." The unicorn answered. Sensing her eager curiosity, Talon began to speak. "Faraway and Earth were one and the same, but that was a long time ago, before humans gave up magic for technology. This in itself was not so terrible a thing but when they gave up all of the magical

sciences they also gave up all of the wonder magic brings. When that happened humans were no longer able to see or interact with any of the magical folks. That caused the world to split apart, creating two worlds, The Human world and The Land of Faraway."

Talon sighed, pausing before continuing in a low and sad voice. "It was a very sad time. The magical folks tried everything in our power to rejoin the two worlds, but all of our magic combined could not restore what once was. We were beginning to lose hope that our friendship with humans would ever blossom again, for they could not cross over to our world or we to theirs. Without contact between our two kinds, memory of the magical folk began to fade from human minds, growing weaker day by day. Soon humans began to believe that the weak memories they sometimes had of us, were not memories at all but mere figments of overactive imagination."

Just then the unicorn's voice changed, taking on a note of pleasure. "But just when we were about to give up trying to repair the rift between the two worlds, we discover the most wonderful and amazing thing. There was a bridge still linking our worlds..." The unicorn paused dramatically before continuing. "There was great rejoicing in Faraway that day. All magical folk from every land took part in the celebrations. Such celebrations had not been seen since before our worlds split apart."

Tiesha found herself barely breathing, so rapt with attention and intrigue was she with the story the unicorn was telling.

"This one small bridge was held in place by the children," Talon continued his story to his spellbound audience of one. For the human children had lost none of their sense of wonder, they still believed in magic and magical folks. That was enough to keep that bridge strong, ensuring that our two worlds would never truly separate."

"So that's why only children can come to the Land of Faraway." said Tiesha in understanding.

"Yes, but not all children can cross the bridge from there to here and back," he announced. "In fact, at that time no one could cross that bridge, for it was too fragile to support passage. All the magical folk joined their magic together and tapping into the hearts of the human children we began the hard and slow task of strengthening the bridge. It took us four hundred human years to make the bridge strong enough for anyone to cross into your world and then it took another hundred years of reinforcing it so that the first human child could cross over it to Faraway."

"The magical folk must be very proud. After all that long hard work you were able to accomplish such a fantastic thing," said Tiesha. "Now children can come to Faraway and enjoy its many wonders."

"Proud... I suppose," said the unicorn in a low voice. "Despite our best efforts, we were still unable to make the bridge strong enough for all children to cross over." He continued in a tone that to Tiesha, did not seem to be very satisfied at all. She could plainly hear a note of sadness in his musical voice. "Even though all children can see magical folks, only the very special ones, those who possess enough imagination and true belief in the magical places, can journey to Faraway."

"Well at least you were able to fix it so that some children could come," said Tiesha cheerfully. "And some is a lot better than none."

"You are right," murmured Talon, feeling comforted by Tiesha's words. In a happier tone he said. "Just imagine, once... all humans could see us and we enjoyed each others company as it was meant to be."

"That must have been a very thrilling time," said Tiesha, trying to imagine what it must have been like to be able to spend lots of time in the company of these magical folks. She had only been in the Land of Faraway a short time and she was already having the most amazing time ever.

"It was a time I will always treasure," answered Talon. "But if the Goblin King is not stopped... soon not even those few special children will be able to come to Faraway. Magic is fading rapidly even mine is beginning to grow weak. Soon only the very old magical folk will be able to use magic. Grom must be stopped and soon or not even the oldest of the magical folk, the Dragon King, will be able to use magic."

"What will happen then?" asked Tiesha softly, fearing the answer.

"Well not even a memory of the magical folk will remain in the minds of human children. When that happens, all magic and wonder will also fade from the hearts of children shattering the bridge connecting our worlds. And without our magic, Faraway will simply fade away to nothing." Talon answered with such misery in his voice that Tiesha felt sure he was going to break out in tears.

She had no idea just how desperate things were in this beautiful, magical land. Now that she did, she wanted to help set things right. "I will reach the Dragon King and get his help no matter what." She announced suddenly and with such determination that she startled the unicorn.

"I know you will," said the unicorn. "And I am proud to be your friend." And with that, he began beating his powerful wings harder, flying faster through the sky.

"How come we are flying so high and I feel as warm as if I were on the ground sitting in the sun?" Tiesha suddenly asked.

"Ah a very intelligent question," said Talon, happy to explain the phenomenon to the bright little girl whose courage he found inspiring. "It is magic that keeps you warm. There is a field of energy surrounding my body that is generated by my unihorn. It is called a magical aura. Think of my unihorn as a powerful battery that produces magical energy. My unihorn also absorbs magical energy directly from the Land of Faraway itself, which it then amplifies and turns into unicorn magic. That's the secret of unicorn magic."

"Oh I see," said Tiesha. "It must be fun having magical powers."

"Yes it is," admitted Talon, his voice taking on a note of amusement as he remembered some of the magical pranks he and his playmates had got up to when he was a foal. "The stories I could tell you would make you split your sides in laughter."

"I played many a prank when I first began learning to use my magic. But…" his voice changed becoming very serious and he turned his head to look at her over his shoulder. "Always remember, having magical abilities is first and foremost, a very serious responsibility. Magic should not be used lightly or carelessly."

"Hmmm," murmured Tiesha wondering why the unicorn had chosen to say what he had with such a strange stare, but decided it really held no significant meaning. "I wonder if we might stop for a while, I am getting hungry."

"Sure," said Talon. "I'm beginning to get hungry myself. Hold tight now...we're going down." And with a whoop the unicorn swooped down through the clouds towards the ground below, causing Tiesha to squeal with delight. Her stomach was doing flip-flops just as if she were on a fast roller coaster.

CHAPTER FOUR

In the Clutches of Goblins

After lunching on some of the food from Tiesha's bag and a variety of berries Talon found growing on bushes close to the small clearing where he had landed, they were ready to resume their journey.

Once they were back in the air Tiesha leaned forward and asked. "How far is it to the Dragon King's kingdom?"

"Let's see. It's through Goblin-Kin Dale, past the Centaur forest, beyond Sprite Valley, over Troll Bridge, then across Goblin kingdom where the Goblin King dwells. After that it's just a short distance through Fire forest, around Harpy hill and across Mer-sprite lagoon," said Talon. "If all goes well, we should be there in two shakes of a sparrow's tail or two dreaming times."

At first Tiesha did not understand what the unicorn meant by two dreaming times. She was about to ask him but then made up her mind to try to figure out by herself what two dreaming times meant. She thought about it carefully. People dreamed when they slept and you usually slept at night. Then that must mean that one dreaming time was one night, and two dreaming times meant two nights.

To test her theory, Tiesha asked Talon if two dreaming times meant two nights.

"Why yes," replied the unicorn with a toss of his mane. "It is two nights."

Tiesha smiled, feeling very pleased. It was just as mommy and daddy always reminded her. If you had enough patience, and put enough thought into solving a problem, you would eventually succeed in solving it.

"Is two days going to be enough time to reach the Dragon King, deliver our message and gain his help before the Goblin King's machines reach Fief?" Tiesha inquired solemnly.

"Of course," said Talon. "The Dragon King has the most powerful magic of all the magical folk of Faraway. He can transport us back to the kingdom of Fief in the twinkling of an eye. He will surely vanquish the Goblin King easily. Get ready. We have arrived at Goblin dale. The sky here is too full of noxious fumes to fly through. We'll have to land soon and continue our travel by ground."

Indeed the sky was becoming a nasty sooty color and Tiesha was beginning to find it quite difficult to breathe. Talon continued flying through the sky for as long as they could breathe the air up there, but eventually the sky became too dark to see and too thick with smoke to breathe without coughing. They were forced from the sky.

Talon swooped down on his powerful wings to land on the mucky ground below.

"Hmmm! It will be tricky going but I believe I can still run in this muck," said Talon taking a few experimental steps.

And so saying he took off in as quick a trot as he could manage in the sludgy mud. As they traveled, Tiesha kept glancing about, alert for any signs of an ambush by the goblins she felt sure were about. For a long time they traveled without incident. The goblins it seemed were busy elsewhere. All the same, Tiesha remained alert. Her Sensei, her karate teacher had taught her that she should always be aware of her surroundings and be ready for trouble so that she could run away to safety as soon as it started.

"Is it safe for us to be traveling goblin lands on the ground and in daylight?" asked Tiesha finally. "Maybe we should find someplace to hide until its night and then continue our travel to the Dragon King's land."

"No, we must continue going, every minute we delay means the Goblin King's great machines get closer to the Elfin-faer's village," explained Talon. "Besides, no goblin can catch me, on the ground or in the air."

At that very moment, there arose a great wailing noise and four nasty looking, big eared goblins leapt up from beneath the mud where they had been hiding, lying in wait for unwary travelers.

"Now we shall take you trespassers to our king," said the biggest goblin in a loud growl as gooey mud slid off him and his companions.

At first Tiesha thought it strange that the mud did not seem able to cling to the goblins or their clothes but quickly decided that it must be goblin magic at work.

"Yes," agreed the companions of the lead goblin. "We'll take you to our king and he will certainly imprison you in the dungeon beneath his castle. Ha, ha, ha!"

"Yes," the lead goblin smirked nastily. "You'll certainly enjoy the dank dark dungeon."

"I don't think that we shall accept your invitation, ruffians. We have an important appointment to keep," said Talon, and with a mighty leap into the air, sailed clear above the heads of the startled goblins.

Landing in the muck, he took off at a fast gallop, the goblins, recovered from their surprise, in hot pursuit on their thick muscular legs. Tiesha looked back over her shoulder at the shouting goblins chasing after them with clubs waving in the air.

"Those mean goblins are running pretty fast, this slippery mud doesn't seem to be slowing them down at all." Tiesha commented.

"Have no fear. They can't hope to outrun a fleet footed unicorn." Talon laughed scornfully. "They will never catch us!"

At that very moment Talon slipped in the muck, tripped and fell. Tiesha sailed off the unicorn's back, right over his head. She flew towards the mud but just like in her karate class, she tucked her head under her arms as she landed on the ground, rolling forward in the direction of her momentum. "Yuck," she muttered as she rolled right up onto her feet. "My new jumpsuit is covered in mud."

She was just about to ask if Talon was all right from his fall when she heard his voice cry out from behind her. "Tiesha run!"

She spun around in time to see the four goblins pulling tight a large net they had thrown over the silver unicorn. She had to help him she decided, but how she had no idea.

Seeing the way she looked at him, the unicorn knew that Tiesha wanted to help him but knew he could not allow her to try, for if she were to be captured too, the mission to the Dragon King would be over. So he called out to her in his most commanding voice.

"Tiesha run! You cannot help me! You have to get away, quickly, while the goblins are too busy with me to chase after you. Remember the Elfin-faer, indeed all of Faraway, is depending on you to reach the Dragon King for his help. Beyond that hill is the woodlands of the lightening sprite once you reach it the goblins will not dare follow you. Besides they will not harm me, they only want to stop us from going on. Now go! Go!"

"I promise I will be back to help you," Tiesha shouted to him. And with one last determined glance at her captured friend, Tiesha took off for the hills as fast as she could run.

She was panting by the time she reached the top of the hill and plunged down the other side and into a stand of trees. When she finally stopped running to catch her breath, she found herself in a thick white fog. The fog made her feel damp and cold. Narrowing her eyes in a squint, Tiesha peered about, trying her best to see in the fog. Fortunately, she was soon able to make out a large thick bush off to her right. The bush seemed to be almost inviting. If she huddled inside it, she might be able to stay warm. The bush would also make a good hiding place from the goblins who she expected to come chasing after her at any moment. She could already hear their howls in the distance coming closer.

Holding the branches apart Tiesha climbed quickly but carefully inside, making sure she did not cut herself on any of the sharp branches. Soon she was sitting safely in the large hollow space inside the bush.

Hearing footsteps Tiesha pushed a leafy branch aside, peering out the small opening she had made. Pretty soon she saw two goblins pass right by the bush, unaware it was her hiding place. Her heart was thumping so loudly in her chest she felt sure the goblins would hear it. As quietly as possible, she slowly let the branch she was holding ease back into place, closing the opening in the bush.

A short while later, she thought she heard a strange yelp but could not be sure. Feeling thirsty from her long run, she took a drink from her squirt water bottle and settled down to wait until the goblins had given up searching for her.

CHAPTER FIVE

A Shocking Meeting

As Tiesha sat sipping the cool water she had time to think and realized what a difficult task laid ahead of her. She had no idea what she should do next. Talon had been captured, leaving her alone to find the Dragon King's kingdom. Without someone to guide her, how would she be able to find her way through the lands of Faraway to the kingdom of the Dragon King? Besides, she was pretty sure that she could not walk all the way to the Dragon King's land in two days. She had to find help, but from where and from whom? Aside from the Elfin-faer queen and the unicorn she did not know anyone in Faraway.

"From whom are we hiding?" asked a squeaky voice in her ear.

Tiesha gave a start and turned her head to see who was in the bush with her. She immediately recognized the thin creature that was only half her size, as a sprite from pictures in her books of magical stories. Unlike the sprites in her storybooks, however, the air seemed to be shimmering around this sprite, producing a hum that reminded Tiesha of the electricity you feel in the air during a lightning storm.

"Oh hi, my name's Tiesha," said Tiesha to the little sprite. "I'm hiding from some nasty goblins that were chasing me."

"Oh they are nasty creatures to be sure," said the sprite with a smile. "But then… I can be sooo much nastier." And to prove his point, the sprite reached out a finger touching Tiesha on the arm. Instantly there was a crackling sound and Tiesha felt an unpleasant electric shock leap through her.

"Oww," exclaimed Tiesha in pain. Rubbing her arm she said. "What was that for?"

"What was what for?" asked the sprite, an expression of innocence on his face.

"That shock you gave me," answered Tiesha, wondering whether or not to believe his innocent expression. Maybe he really was unaware he had shocked her.

"Oh that, it's what I do, I am Buzz, the lightening sprite," the diminutive sprite smiled, puffing up his chest like a peacock. "My magic generates electrical charges which I can use to shock others. That's how I chased away those goblins a short while ago. It's how I protect my woodlands."

"Well, Buzz," said Tiesha. "Thank you for chasing the goblins away but please try to be more careful, your electric shock really stung."

"Oh it wasn't an accident. I shocked you on purpose," Buzz said with a cruel smirk. "You're in my forest and I didn't invite you to come here. So I'm going to keep shocking you until you leave."

And with that he shocked her again.

"Hey... Stop," cried Tiesha, "You're being mean!"

"I know," laughed the Sprite.

The sprite kept touching her with the tip of a finger, each time giving her mild but very annoying electrical shocks. After each shock she tried to speak but the mischievous little sprite would only shock her again, causing her to vibrate so hard that her teeth chattered together.

Unable to speak, Tiesha finally gave up trying. Gritting her teeth together, she raised her water bottle. Giving it a hard squeeze, she sprayed the sprite with water. There was a sizzling sound as a dazzling display of sparkles exploded all over the sprite's body. Tiesha had to close her eyes, so bright were the sparks.

As the sparks frizzled and flew, Buzz hopped around in the cramped space inside the bush, yelping in pain. Finally the sparks stopped flying and the sprite fell on his behind.

"Oww!" he complained in a loud indignant voice. "That was not very nice."

"Well, it wasn't very nice of you to keep shocking me either," said Tiesha in her most stern tone. "You shouldn't go around shocking people with your electrical magic, you know!"

"And why not?" growled Buzz, his voice sounding petulant as he glared up at Tiesha from the ground.

"Because it's a very cruel thing to do, that's why." Tiesha explained in a patient voice, as if she were speaking to her baby brother Kyrel. "After all, you didn't like it when the water caused you to shock yourself, did you?"

"No I didn't," admitted the sprite ruefully. "It hurt all over! But these are my woods and I don't like people traveling through them, I only shock them to make them stay away. And it has worked very well so far. Everyone knows not to travel these woods."

"Why ever do you want everyone to stay away from such beautiful woods?" asked Tiesha curiously. "Shouldn't the woods be a place for everyone to come and enjoy nature? It's selfish to want to keep the woods to yourself."

"I'm not selfish!" The sprite objected in a loud voice.

"It seems selfish to me." said Tiesha, folding her arms.

"What do you know," he grumbled. "I'm not trying to keep the woodlands to myself. I'm only protecting it."

"Oh really?" said Tiesha in a tone of disbelief.

"Yes really. People are nasty creatures who litter, trample the flowers and damage the trees. It's my job to protect these woods of my ancestors," said Buzz puffing up his chest with pride. "And that's what I do!"

"I wonder if you have ever talked to any of the people before you start shocking them?" asked Tiesha.

"Err...well no," admitted Buzz.

"Then how do you know all the people who visit would damage the woods?" demanded Tiesha.

"Err…Err...well because my father said so, as his father told him," answered the sprite.

"Ok…Ok I get it," said Tiesha. "But I'm sure your dad did not shock people as soon as he met them. Didn't he at least find out if they meant to damage the woods first?"

"Well, yes he did do that," answered Buzz. "But he always ended up shocking everyone anyway. So I decided to save myself some time and shock them first."

"So you never give anyone a chance to show you that they might not be the kind of person who would destroy your woods?" said Tiesha reproachfully.

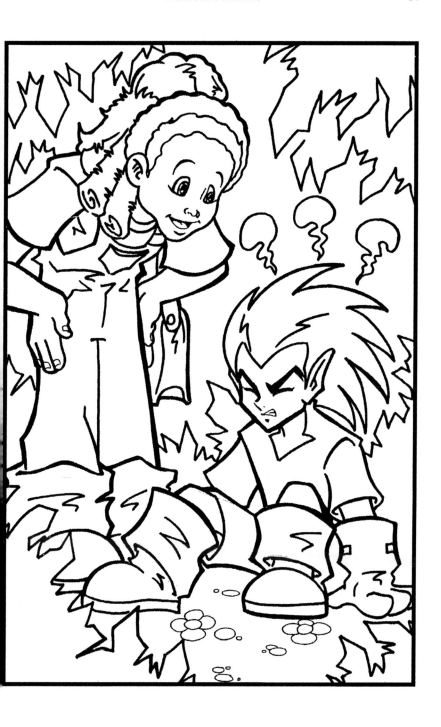

"Err… no," he answered softly, hanging his head in embarrassment.

"I guess you don't have many friends do you?" said Tiesha quietly.

"Come to think of it, I don't have any friends. Not since I took over as protector of the woodlands." Buzz answered, in a pitiful tone of voice.

"Did you ever think that maybe you don't have any friends because you never take the time to talk to anyone before you so cruelly shock them. Maybe if you tried talking to people instead of hurting them, you would find out that not everyone intends to do your woods harm. At least you might finally meet a friend." said Tiesha. "Anyway I have to go now."

"Wait!" cried the sprite as Tiesha began parting the bush to get out.

"What do you want?" Tiesha asked, turning her head to look at him.

"Don't go yet." Buzz pleaded. "I am really very sorry that I shocked you."

"Apology accepted," said Tiesha after a moment of thought. Smiling she said. "See… it does not hurt to be nice or polite."

"If I promised not to shock you, or go around shocking anyone else, unless it's necessary, would you be my friend?" Buzz asked eagerly.

"I don't see why not," Tiesha answered.

"Good," smiled Buzz delightedly. "Maybe you could stay for a while. I could show you around my woodlands. I'm sure you would like it here."

"I'm sure I would," Tiesha smiled at him. "But I'm on my way to ask for the Dragon King's help to stop the Goblin King before he destroys all the forests of Faraway."

"Someone's destroying the forests of Faraway?" breathed the sprite in shock.

"Yes, the Goblin King and his great machines," Tiesha answered.

"Hmm," murmured the sprite. "That explains why the sky has become so dark lately and why the woodlands seem to be wilting."

"The magical power of all the magic folk I've met so far is beginning to fade." said Tiesha. "Has yours been affected as well?"

"I have noticed that my electrical magic takes a bit longer to recharge," answered Buzz. Leaping to his feet he declared. "My duty is clear, I must help you. I know all the lands of Faraway. I can get you to the land of the Dragon King in no time at all."

Tiesha could hardly believe it. She had found help! "Why thank you. That's very nice of you to offer your help."

"It's what a friend would do and I would like to make up for shocking you," he smiled. A moment later his smile turned into a wide grin and he added. "Besides I love adventures and this will be a great one."

After Buzz stuffed an item he said they would need on the journey into his glove, the new friends started out across the sprite's woodlands, heading toward the north.

CHAPTER SIX

Honey-Spiced Berries

Along the way, Tiesha told Buzz what she had learned about the Goblin King from the Elfin-faer queen and Talon, the unicorn. He tried his best to comfort her about her friend's capture. He got so angry at the Goblin King's misdeeds that sparks flew from his hair. He vowed to do all in his power to defeat the villain and stop the destruction of Faraway.

Later, Buzz asked Tiesha to tell him all about the human world. She told him all about Canada, where she lived. She told him about her friends, her school and her neighborhood. She told him about Barbados, the Bahamas and America where some of her relatives live and she had visited. Buzz thought that the human world sounded like an amazing fun place. He became very excited and asked if he could visit Tiesha and have her show him around her world some time.

"Of course," said Tiesha, with a playful smile. "That would be nice. But we would have to hide your ears and you would have to promise not to use any magic."

"No magic," said Buzz in an injured tone. "Why that's like asking me not to eat honey-spiced berries."

"I have never had honey-spiced berries," said Tiesha. "In fact I don't think I have ever heard of them before, so I am pretty sure we don't have any in our world."

"You don't have honey-spiced berries," breathed Buzz disbelievingly. "Why they are the most delicious berries in the world. Surely they must grow everywhere."

"Not in the human world I'm afraid," Tiesha told him.

"That's too bad, honey-spiced berries are a treat that should not be missed," said Buzz feeling sorry that his new friend had never had the chance to enjoy the tasty treat.

The sprite's face suddenly brightened and he said. "Well lucky for you I am your guide and traveling companion because the shortcut over this hill leads to a honey-spice berry woods. And honey-spiced berries are always in season so we will be able to pick as many as we like for you to enjoy."

"That would be wonderful, I am beginning to get hungry again," smiled Tiesha.

"Then let's hurry." Buzz smiled, picking up the pace.

They had almost reached the top of the hill when he said in a mischievous tone. "You said I have to refrain from using magic when I visit you in your world right?"

"Yes," answered Tiesha. Noticing the tone in his voice, she wondered what the wily sprite was up to.

"Then I just have to use my magic now as much as I can, so I propose a race to the berry bushes," giggled Buzz rubbing his hands together and producing a soft crackle of electricity. "And to make things interesting," he began.

Before he could finish his statement, Tiesha exclaimed. "Oh you wouldn't dare!"

The mischievous gleam in his eyes only got brighter as Tiesha wagged a finger beneath his nose. "Of course I would," Buzz laughed, raising a finger into the air, electrical magic sparking on the tip. "I'm going to get you. Hehehe! I promise they will only be little shocks, you'll hardly feel them."

"Well you'll have to catch me first," yelled Tiesha, and with a laugh of her own, she took off in a fast sprint, racing to the top of the hill and down the other side.

"I'm going to get you, oh I'm going to get you," sang the sprite giving chase.

Being able to run far faster than almost anyone, the little sprite did his best to run as slowly as possible, allowing Tiesha to get down the hillside and into the woods before he could catch her.

Reaching the woods Tiesha darted off the path, running in and among the trunks of the big trees. One of the first things she noticed was that there were red berries covered with golden freckles on bushes growing everywhere among the trees. She had no time to pick any of them before Buzz came running into the woods, singing out as he came.

"Now I have you. Prepare to be shocked!"

Laughing Tiesha ducked down behind a bush, but the sprite saw her and fired an electrical bolt into the bush, chasing her out. That began the game in earnest. Every time she ducked behind a tree Buzz would fire a weak charge of electricity at her, deliberately missing. Squealing in delight she would yell out. "Ha-ha missed me!" Then she would race off to hide again.

Buzz would then pipe up. "Oh yeah? Well I'll get you with the next one." And in a shot he would be off, chasing her.

The two had such a good time playing among the trees chasing each other that they forgot all about the passage of time and played until they were both too tired to continue running. Laughing they collapsed to the ground beneath a particularly big tree right next to a large honey-spiced berry bush. After catching his breath, Buzz aimed his finger at the berry bush and let loose a particularly long stream of magical electricity. The bolt of magic brought a rain of the red golden freckled berries flowing down upon them.

Not waiting for Tiesha, Buzz began picking up berries and stuffing them into his mouth. "Hmmm, these are so good," he mumbled with his mouth full.

Laughing at the sprite, Tiesha picked up a berry, examining it slowly before placing it into her mouth, biting into it. Her face lit up with pure delight at the wonderful taste of the berry. It had to be the best tasting berry she had ever had in her life. With a giggle she began stuffing berries into her mouth almost as fast as the sprite.

"Wow, these are soooo good!" she managed to mutter as she munched on the sweet berries. "You were right about the taste."

"Told you," Buzz managed to say through a mouth full of berries.

After they had eaten their fill of berries, the two friends sat slouched against the trunk of the tree, faces beaming with contentment.

"It is beginning to get dark, we had better find shelter for the night," said Tiesha.

"Don't worry I know the perfect place," said Buzz. "I use to spend a lot of time exploring these woods whenever I came to pick berries. Come on I will show you."

The sprite groaned as he climbed to his feet. "I think I might have eaten too many berries."

"Yes," agreed Tiesha, struggling to her feet as well. "I am so full I feel as if I am going to burst."

Together the two companions waddled along a well-worn path through the trees, joking about berry bushes growing from their tummies. Buzz led them to a giant tree growing in the middle of the woods. It was becoming pretty dark at this time, so it was only when they got right up to the tree that Tiesha noticed a small sprite size door set right into the tree trunk.

"Ta-daa!" Buzz said, bowing to Tiesha and gesturing to the door. "I give you the Buzz living-tree Inn. Good one right?"

"Wow," was all Tiesha could say as she stared at the tree house. It was absolutely enchanting. The tree trunk was as big around as a regular house and the door looked as if it had been carved right into it, but it did not seem to have harmed the tree at all.

"My dad and I are going to build a tree house but it's not going to be like this," said Tiesha to Buzz. "Our tree houses are usually built up among the branches of the tree. I might have known that a tree house in Faraway would be more fantastic."

"Oh we have as many kinds of tree houses as there are tree and wood sprites... And there are a lot of them," explained Buzz with a little laugh. "My cousins are tree sprites. This is one of their homes. They go from woodland to woodland all around Faraway, tending the trees, keeping them healthy. They are usually in one of the woodlands further south at this time of year, so the tree house here is empty. We will have it all to ourselves."

Walking right up to the door Buzz said. "Hello tree, its Buzz, would you open up for me please."

There was a rustling up among the branches of the tree that sounded to Tiesha as if the tree had returned the greeting of the little sprite. Then the door in the tree trunk opened invitingly.

"Tree remembers me even after all this time," Buzz chuckled. And with a light pat on the tree trunk the sprite stepped through the door into the tree.

Tiesha had to bend over to get through the door but once

inside she found that she could stand upright. The hollow inside
the tree was wide and spacious; extending upward so far overhead
that Tiesha could not see any ceiling above. There were tiny chairs,
tables and cots set out around the room. The house-tree was so warm
and cozy Tiesha became aware of just how tired she was.

Buzz walked across the room and jumped up onto one of the
small beds. "See, I make a great traveling companion."

"Yes you do," agreed Tiesha, climbing onto one of the small
beds. "These beds remind me of my brother's crib." The sprite
sized bed was a little short for Tiesha, so she had to arrange herself
carefully so she could fit on it. She curled up on her side so that her
feet would not dangle over the bottom of the bed.

Tiesha was so tired that she was fast asleep almost as soon as
her head touched the pillow. Smiling, Buzz got up and went over to
Tiesha's bed pulling the blanket up to cover her sleeping form.

"Sleep well my new friend and happy dreams."

Climbing back into his bed he closed his eyes and fell
asleep.

-CHAPTER SEVEN-

It's Scary in Howling Hollow

The two friends awoke and set out from the tree house early in the morning, both eager to resume their journey after getting such a good night's sleep. For breakfast they picked and snacked on different kinds of fruits, Buzz making sure to teach Tiesha the names of each one. He always seemed to have a funny story to accompany the name of each fruit. Tiesha found herself liking the little sprite more and more as she got to know him better. He was really not as naughty as she had at first thought on meeting him, she realized. He was just a tad overzealous in protecting his forest.

They had just crossed a big clearing and were just about to enter another set of trees when Buzz suddenly stopped talking, coming to a halt. For a moment he remained quiet; then with a sigh he said softly. "Now we come to the Land of Howling Hollow."

"That sounds scary," said Tiesha trying to peer through the trees.

"It can be," said the sprite in a dramatic whisper. "But we have to go through it if we hope to reach the Dragon King in time."

"So we go through," said Tiesha. "But first tell me why they call it Howling Hollow."

Buzz sighed again. "It is the home of the Howlers, who are by far the strangest of the magic folk in all of Faraway. And I do mean strange. Why just imagine spending all of your time racing around and howling at the moon."

"Well I guess we had better get going," said Tiesha trying to sound braver than she felt.

"You're right," said Buzz in a small voice. "Besides I've never heard of the Howlers being dangerous. But then again that might be because everyone stays away from Howling Hollow." The sprite made no move to go ahead.

"Didn't you say everyone stayed away from your woodlands?" Tiesha chuckled nervously. "And you're not dangerous."

"I am fearsome," Buzz protested indignantly.

"Then we have nothing to fear from the Howlers," said Tiesha, stepping forward towards the dark woods. "So come on."

As Tiesha took another slow step forward, Buzz shrugged and walked past her into the woods. Swallowing a sudden lump in her throat Tiesha followed him.

Walking side by side the two friends walked along a narrow path through the trees. The wood was very dark and gloomy, the gnarled trees casting patches of deep dark shadows everywhere. At first both the sprite and the little girl spoke to each other in loud voices, which made them feel comforted and brave as they tried to cross through the scary wood as quickly as possible. They were both taking care not to look into the patches of shadows because they were afraid that their imaginations would run away with them.

"What do they look like?" asked Tiesha.

"Who?" Buzz grunted.

"You know... the Howlers." Tiesha continued. "Have you ever seen one?"

"No," said Buzz. "I've never seen a Howler. But I've been told that they are big and covered in fur, with very long mouths. They are very strong and can run fast. They never ever leave Howling Hollow, not even to attend the great festival of the magic folks."

"They don't sound very social," murmured Tiesha.

"They are not... at least that's what I heard," said Buzz. "Why they don't even let the tree sprites tend their trees."

"I hope we get out of these woods soon," said Tiesha. "It's really creepy here."

"We're almost there, only a short distance to go and we'll be out of these woods," said Buzz. "When we reach the end of Howling Hollow we will be in the glorious sunlight again."

At the moment the air was suddenly rend by the most horrific howl the two had ever heard, startling them so much that they jumped and huddled closer together. They began looking around with identical expressions of alarm on their faces.

"Wh...What was that?" asked Tiesha not even trying to keep

the quaver from her voice.

"It...it must be a Howler," answered Buzz in a voice that sounded just as nervous as Tiesha's.

"Do they sound close to you?" she asked Buzz, looking around warily.

At that moment another horrifying howl rend the air. This time it sounded as if it had come from very close by them, causing them both to look up into the shadowy branches of the trees. What they saw gave them quite a start. A pair of big yellowy eyes stared down at them from the shadows in the tree branches.

The low rustling sounds of movement coming from among the trees all around them caused the two friends to look around. Many pairs of big yellowy eyes stared at them from every patch of shadow that could be seen.

"I don't like the looks of those eyes," hissed Tiesha in a low whisper.

"Nor do I," Buzz whispered back. "I don't think they like us being here."

Before they could say anything else, the woods erupted into a chorus of loud howling.

"Run!" shouted Tiesha, taking off as fast as her legs could carry her.

Buzz caught up to her easily, running and pointing a finger back behind him and letting loose sizzling bolts of magical electricity as rapidly as he could. Some of the howling turned to howls of pain, showing that at least some of his bolts were hitting the Howlers.

They did not stop running until they burst out of the woods and reached the top of the hill that lay just beyond Howling Hollow. Bending over and supporting themselves on their knees, they stared back down the hill at the woods as they caught their breaths.

"That was close," said Tiesha. "I thought we were going to be caught by those... whatever they really are."

"Oh we were fine," Buzz smiled. "You should have seen the look on your face. I never knew humans could run so fast. Hahaha."

"Oh yeah... well you should have seen your face too," said Tiesha. "And you were the one screaming."

"I was not!" Buzz stopped laughing. "Was I?"

Tiesha stared hard at the sprite then fell to the ground laughing. "Hahahah... You should see your face now."

In a moment Buzz joined her, rolling around as he laughed hysterically. After the two friends were finished laughing in relief they decided to get on with their quest. They crossed the lands of Rockilytes without incident, never even seeing any of the big boulder-like people. In the land of Small, where every thing was, as to be expected, small, they were treated to a picnic meal of many kinds of tiny breads and cakes, fruits and fruit beverages by the Faraway folk who lived there, the Llittle. The people, who were only knee high, and all dressed in brightly colored clothes and strangely shaped hats, told Tiesha that they were relatives of the Wee-kin. The two traveling companions had a great time with the Llittle before they had to start out on their journey again.

CHAPTER EIGHT

Crossing a Troll Bridge

As they marched along between rows and rows of low rolling hills Buzz said. "This land we are about to enter, belong to the Centaurs."

"Well after Howling Hollow, I certainly hope they are friendly." said Tiesha.

"Actually centaurs can be pretty nasty if they don't like you, but have no fear, I will protect you," boasted Buzz, puffing up his chest, an expression of smug confidence on his face.

"Oh like you protected me against the Howlers, right?" said Tiesha snidely, folding her arms and looking down on the sprite in bemusement.

Ignoring her, Buzz said. "I'm more powerful than any centaur."

"Yeah... sure you are..." said Tiesha with a laugh.

"Of course I am. In fact," Buzz continued boasting. "I'm more powerful than all the races of the lands of Faraway."

"Buzz!" said Tiesha, pretending to be stern, staring down at the sprite as she began tapping one foot on the ground.

"Well... except for maybe the Dragon King and the Goblin King," Buzz mused. "Hmm... almost forgot the Elfin-faer queen and maybe the Unicorn king."

"Buzz!" said Tiesha again.

"Ok... ok I guess there are also the Howlers," admitted the sprite, "and maybe the Centaur Empress." Then, staring down at his feet, he added in a smaller voice. "And then there are the harpies and not to mention the..." he stopped speaking for a moment, looking a little downcast. "You know, when you think about it, there are a lot of powerful magic folk in Faraway." Then like a ray of sunshine his face brightened up, and he was cheerful once more. "But then again

I'm young and still maturing."

Buzz puffed up his chest again, placing his hands on his waist and holding his head high, he declared. "So I'll be more powerful than the lot of them when I grow up."

Tiesha could not hold back her laughter any longer. Buzz really knew how to get her laughing. His naughty nature went hand in hand with his sense of amusement. She was very glad to have met him even if it had got her a few shocks.

Then in a more serious tone, Buzz said. "We have to be very careful if we meet a centaur. They are unpredictable. And they are usually not very hospitable."

"You mean they are a lot like you," said Tiesha with an amused chuckle.

After a moment's hesitation Buzz laughed and said. "Yup they are exactly like me, so they might decide to be nasty first and talk after."

"And that..." said a gruff voice. "Is just what I intend to do!"

From behind a tree stepped a huge centaur giving them both a start of fright. Tiesha was aghast. This creature was by far more imposing than the goblins she had ran away from earlier. She looked around quickly but there was no where to run to, they were cornered. She decided to try a different tact.

"Hello," said Tiesha bravely. "I'm Tiesha and this is my friend Buzz, the sprite."

"I certainly don't care who you are," said the centaur. "You're on Centaur ground, so you must pay the price for trespassing uninvited. However, as this is your first offence, human, I will let you off easy, just so long as you pay tribute to the Centaur Empress."

"Well," said Tiesha, holding up a hand to silence Buzz's indignant retort. "That certainly seems fair. But if you don't mind... what exactly is a tribute?"

"You mean to tell me that you don't know what a tribute is?" growled the centaur, deepening his scowl even more.

"Well! I'm only a little girl after all," said Tiesha smiling sweetly. "What is it?"

"Why...why...why that's...that's..." The centaur stuttered,

staring down at her innocent expression and beguiling smile. Then he suddenly broke into a belly-shaking laugh. "Hohohohohoho!"

"You are indeed a little tyke of a girl," he managed to say between gusts of laughter. "And what a precious one at that. I think that in this case we can waive the tribute. I'm sure the Empress will understand."

The centaur's roaring laughter was so infectious that Tiesha and Buzz found themselves joining in. After the laughter had died away, the centaur spoke in his deep growling voice. This time however, his tone was softer and friendlier. "So you're the special girl queen Gossamer brought from the human world to help stop the Goblin King."

"How did you know about that?" asked Tiesha.

"Well there is little the centaurs don't know," he began, "especially me, Fagan." He laughed again. "The Elfin-faer queen chose well, for already you have crossed the goblin's homeland escaping capture, befriended the fleet footed and equally quick tempered electric sprite. And that's no small feat indeed."

"Hey what do you mean quick tempered?" exclaimed Buzz. "I'm very even- tempered."

Smiling, the centaur continued as the sprite grumbled in a low mutter. "And after doing many more equally impressive things in your adventures so far, you have gained the admiration of Fagan the Grim. With such talents, you will surely win your way to the Dragon King."

"I certainly intend to," smiled Tiesha. "And with Buzz's help, I know I will."

Buzz beamed when he heard his friend's statement, it made him feel proud to hear Tiesha's great confidence in him.

Chuckling, the centaur said. "Well there's no love lost between the centaurs and the goblins so I might as well do my bit to help. Come, I'll escort you across centaur land. It's a long journey and you look tired. Hop up onto my back, both of you."

Realizing that she was tired, Tiesha took him up on his offer, hopping up onto his back. Buzz elected to walk saying that he never got tired. On the long journey, Tiesha listened to the centaur's description of the lands she and Buzz still had to cross.

Fagan decided to entertain them with stories as they traveled. After a while his booming voice and rolling gait lulled Tiesha into a deep sleep. When she awakened much later, she felt refreshed. She was surprised to discover they had already arrived at the Troll-bridge she had to win passage over.

"This is as far as I can take you," said Fagan. "Now listen carefully. You will have to trick the troll into giving you safe passage."

"Crossing the bridge will be no problem for us," bragged Buzz. "Even carrying Tiesha I will be able to speed right by the dim witted troll before he knows it."

"Yes, I have no doubt that normally you would be able to speed past him before he even knew you were there," agreed Fagan. "But your magic would have to be working properly, and if centaur magic already grows undependable then surely the magic of the younger magic folk such as you, must also be growing weaker."

Buzz concentrated for a moment then without a word he pushed both hands into his pockets and hung his head, all in all, a good indication that the centaur was right in his assessment of the sprites magical powers.

"Are you okay?" asked Tiesha in alarm, feeling concern for her friend.

"Oh I'm fine," Buzz answered quickly, not wanting to cause his friend to worry unduly. "I am just feeling a little less charged than usual… I guess my magic is beginning to grow weaker."

"Ok, said the Fagan. "Here's what you should do to get across safely."

After listening to what the centaur had to say, they were ready to face the troll. Tiesha and the sprite approached the bridge walking slowly, whistling a jaunty tune as if they had not a care in the world. When they were almost upon the bridge, a large hairy troll jumped out from under it, barring their way.

"You can't cross my bridge, it's forbidden." The troll growled nastily.

"Why is it forbidden?" asked Tiesha innocently.

"Because it just is," roared the troll. "Be gone before I put you in my dinner pot."

"Okay, we'll go back," said Tiesha.

"But if we don't cross, the bridge how will we get the tools we need to dig up the treasur…" began Buzz.

As quick as can be, Tiesha jabbed her elbow into his ribs, interrupting what he had been saying.

"Ooww!" he exclaimed, rubbing his ribs and glaring at her.

"Shhhh!" she hissed at him. "That's supposed to be a secret."

"Oops… I forgot," said the sprite trying his best to look crestfallen and almost not succeeding.

"Did you say treasure?" asked the troll eagerly, leaning forward attempting to smile but only succeeding in looking more like he was snarling.

"Err, no!" said both Tiesha and Buzz hastily.

"Oh yes you did," insisted the troll stepping closer to them. Lowering his voice to a friendly pitch, he said. "You said treasure. I heard you as plain as day."

"Oh no," said Tiesha. "You must have misheard what my friend said. We know nothing about treasure hidden in a grove of trees on the centaur's side of the bridge."

"Ah ha!" exclaimed the greedy troll, rubbing his hands together, his eyes shining. "So you do know of treasure hidden in a grove of trees over there."

"Of course not," piped up Buzz. "We have absolutely no knowledge of any treasure hidden around here."

"Tell you what," said the troll in his friendliest voice. "I really like you two, you remind me of my own niece and nephew. You surely do. I believe we can be very good friends, so I'm willing to let you cross my bridge. Friends should help each other, right?"

"That's true," agreed Tiesha. "Friends should help friends whenever possible."

"I quite agree," said Buzz.

"That's right," said the troll quickly, hoping his greed did not show in his eyes. "Tell you what. I'll let you cross my bridge to get your digging tools. Then I could guard the spot where the treasure is until you got back. And once it's dug up, we can share it like friends would. What do you say my cute little friends?"

"Well I don't know," said Tiesha, slowly rubbing at her pursed lips thoughtfully.

"Think about it, those centaurs are a shifty lot. They might steal the treasure once you have gone to get the tools." The troll did his best to speak earnestly. "With me around, they wouldn't dare attempt to take the treasure."

"Who's to say that when we're gone, you won't steal the treasure," said Buzz.

"I would never do that to my friends," said the troll indignantly. Tell you what, you don't have to tell me where the treasure is, only the area close to it where I should stand guard. As a show of good faith, I'll even let you cross the bridge before you tell me where to stand guard."

"I believe we can trust him," said Buzz turning to Tiesha. "He seems a nice enough troll."

"Okay," she said to the troll. "We'll tell you once we are on the other side of the bridge."

The troll let them pass rubbing his hands together eagerly. Once they had reached the other side, they directed him to stand guard by a particular area of the forest close to the centaur border. Waving goodbye, they moved on. Once they were out of sight of the Troll Bridge, the sprite began to laugh.

"Ha, ha, ha," laughed Buzz rolling around on the ground. "I can't believe that stupid troll was so greedy he fell for such an old trick."

Tiesha was laughing so hard, her sides hurt. "My mom always said greed makes people do foolish things."

"Well your mom was right," laughed the sprite. "I wonder how long it'll take for him to figure out he has been tricked."

"It doesn't matter, we'll be halfway to the Dragon Kingdom by then," laughed Tiesha. "Let's get going."

Still chuckling, their spirits lifted by the entire episode, the two companions skipped along arm in arm. They traveled onward, still laughing at the foolish greedy troll.

CHAPTER NINE

Turning Up the Heat

After what seemed like hours of walking Tiesha and Buzz topped the crest of a rolling hill and were treated to a breath taking sight. Spread out below was a stretch of red sand with hundreds of small rainbows hanging in the air just above the sand.

"It's beautiful," breathed Tiesha. She had never seen anything like this before. Not only were there rainbows as far as the eye could see but these rainbows seem to have colors Tiesha had never seen before or had any name for.

"Yes," answered Buzz. "This land is very beautiful but also very dangerous. This place is usually avoided even more than Howling Hollow."

"Why?" asked Tiesha. "It's so beautiful."

Buzz turned to look at her, his expression was more serious than Tiesha had ever seen before. "They avoid it because this is the land of the Fire Imps."

Reaching into his glove Buzz pulled out a little white flower. "I have been saving this for our journey through this land." Holding the flower up to his mouth Buzz blew on it and immediately disappeared.

"Buzz?" breathed Tiesha in near fright. "Hey, where did you go? Buzz?"

"I'm still here," said Buzz's voice, as his hand appeared in the air beside her. "Here take my hand."

Tiesha took his hand and immediately she could see the rest of him. He was smiling.

"Now you are invisible too," he said.

"Invisible?" she breathed softly.

"Yup," he laughed, before beginning his explanation. "The flower's magic can make you invisible for a short time. It should

keep us invisible long enough to cross the Fire Imps' land. But we have to hurry and be careful not to let go of my hand or you'll become visible."

Holding hands they walked as fast as they could, trying to get across the long desert before the flower's magic could wear off. Suddenly they heard a loud whooshing sound and little creatures made entirely of flames surrounded them. Tiesha almost spoke but Buzz stopped her by squeezing her hand, placing a finger to his lips. She nodded to him to show that she understood. Even though the Fire Imps could not see them, they could hear them, so they had to remain silent to stay undetected. The Imps had a head and a body with two arms but no legs. They did not need legs because they floated in the air.

On tiptoes Tiesha and Buzz treaded their way carefully through the floating Fire Imps. The playing Imps had no idea that they were there and the two of them were able to pass by. After they had left the Fire Imps far behind, Buzz breathed a sigh of relief.

"Phew! Did you feel how hot it was with so many Imps flying about? I thought we would catch on fire for sure."

"Shhhh!" hissed Tiesha pointing to another bunch of Imps she had just spotted approaching from the left, floating along on air currents. These Imps' fiery bodies burned more brightly than the other Imps Tiesha and Buzz had already passed by, casting off intense heat that not only made it uncomfortable for the two friends but hard to breath the closer the Imps came to them.

The two of them tried to walk faster, careful to remain silent but this time the Fire Imps seemed to be keeping pace with them. After this had gone on for a long while, Buzz spoke in the quietest whisper he could manage in Tiesha's ear. "I think the magic is beginning to wear off. The Fire Imps may be able to partially see us but not well enough to tell we are people, at least not yet."

"How long will it be before they can tell?" whispered Tiesha.

Just then one of the Fire Imps yelled out. "Aha! I see them better now. Intruders, get them!"

"Never mind!" She breathed.

"Run!" Yelled Buzz, as the Fire Imps began swooping

towards them. Tiesha did not need any urging, she began running as fast as she could.

"This way!" cried Buzz, pulling Tiesha along with him. "We're almost at the land of the giants!"

And just as the Fire Imps got close enough to throw tiny fireballs at them, they saw giant feet ahead. Tiesha looked backed over her shoulder to see how close the Fire Imps were and was surprised to see that they had stopped chasing them. The Imps were just floating in the air spluttering and calling jeers at them but were making no move to come any closer.

They both stopped running, turning to watch the antics of the angry Imps who were shaking fiery fists at them. Buzz shook his fist back and began doing a little dance. "Afraid of the giants are you? Well stay there and fume!"

The Imps threw one last set of fireballs at them but all of them fell well short of their position. After that Tiesha and Buzz set off across the land of the giants. Tiesha asked the sprite why the giants simply ignored them even though they were very careful not to step on their little visitors. Buzz told her that was simply the way of the giants. They had not spoken to anyone but themselves since Faraway had been separated from the world of the humans.

Soon they arrived at the riverbank at the edge of the giants' land. Buzz explained that they needed to find something to float on because they had to follow the little river out to sea. After a quick search they found a thick log tangled in the brush at the river's edge, which they dragged into the river. They cheered as the log floated on the water. Soon the two of them were floating along the river, sitting astride the log eating food from Tiesha's bag.

"This is fun," laughed Tiesha as she munched on her last purple peach. "I really didn't expect to have such an adventure."

"Faraway is a very adventurous place," laughed Buzz. "I hope you come back when the Goblin King has been vanquished and we can just go exploring. There is so much more for you to see. And many more magic folks to be met."

Before Tiesha could answer a loud voice rang out. "There they are! Get them!"

"Whoa?" breathed Tiesha, struggling to keep from falling

off the log, which was bobbing crazily on the water as what seemed to be long thick blades of river grass with grim looking faces rushed through the water towards them.

"Reed folks," answered Buzz also doing his best to stay on the log. "I forgot they are close friends of the goblins." Seeing no way they could escape the Reed folk who were perfectly at home in the water, Buzz grabbed Tiesha around the waist and leapt off the log. "We are gone!"

Landing on the water's surface the sprite called on all his electrical speed and began to run in blur of motion. He was running so fast that he did not sink but was actually running on the surface of the water, carrying Tiesha along with him. Tiesha was amazed, she had no idea that the little sprite could move so fast. In the blink of an eye they had left the Reed folk far behind them and were almost half way down the river.

Just as they thought they were safe, a new group of Reed folk sprang up from beneath the water directly in front of them. Not even slowing down, Buzz swerved around them in a blur. There were almost past the Reed folk, when one of them extended a long leafy arm out, tripping Buzz. Still holding onto Tiesha, the sprite went tumbling forward. Splash, Buzz and Tiesha fell into the water, going beneath the surface. In a moment the two of them surfaced, spluttering and spitting water from their mouths.

"Uh oh," cried Tiesha as she saw the Reed folk bearing down on them.

"We have them now," yelled one of the Reed folk, gleefully reaching out a long arm towards the hapless friends.

Before the leafy arm could reach them a giant hand reached down from the sky, plucking Tiesha and Buzz from the water. Tiesha could hardly believe it, saved by the giants again. "Oh thank you for saving us again," she told the giant.

"You are welcome little human child." A booming voice replied. "Now be on your way. Safe journey." The giant reached all the way out and placed them safely down on the seashore where the river flowed into the sea.

"They actually spoke to you. Wow! Wow! You spoke with giants!" Buzz was beside himself with excitement.

"They saved us... I thanked them." laughed Tiesha. "What's the big deal?"

"Remember what I told you. The giants have not spoken to anyone but giants in centuries!" cried Buzz.

"Oh," breathed Tiesha. "Guess it's a big deal then."

And with that they both began laughing. It felt good to laugh after the tension of their close escapes.

"My cousins the Mer-sprites live in this sea," said Buzz, shaking water from his clothes and hair. "We lost our log but we'll be able to get across the sea."

Placing two fingers in his mouth, he whistled a few high wailing notes. In a few minutes, six heads broke the surface of the water and six Mer-sprites came out of the sea onto the shore. They looked a lot like Buzz but had scales on their skin like fish. They greeted Buzz with warm hugs, happy to see him. Buzz introduced Tiesha, then quickly explained that they were on their way to see the Dragon King and needed his cousins' help to cross the sea. The Mer-sprites began chattering to each other excitedly. Then they leapt into the water, disappearing. A short time later, they returned. This time, however, they had two large dolphins with them.

Soon Tiesha and Buzz were riding on the backs of the dolphins as the beautiful creatures cruised through the water. For the two friends, it was a wonderful experience. The dolphins kept up a whistling speech that Tiesha could not understand but loved hearing anyway. However, Buzz like the Mer-sprites, had no problem understanding the dolphins because they used the same whistling language to communicate.

Buzz used the time to inform Tiesha that once on the island they would be able to use a magical doorway in the cave of blue crystal to transport themselves to the Dragon King's lands in the frozen north. Tiesha felt both elated and relieved to be nearing the end of her journey.

-CHAPTER TEN-

Drago!

The group of travelers had almost reached the other shore when a horrendous noise split the air and two harpies swooped down from the sky trying to grab Tiesha and Buzz off the backs of the swimming dolphins.

"Oh no you don't!" yelled Buzz. Glancing down to make sure his legs were not in the water, he released an electrical charge right at the swooping harpies. The winged creatures yowled in pain, as they were shocked. The harpies broke off their swooping attack, fleeing back up into the sky.

Louder screeching herald the arrival of more harpies as the dolphins brought Tiesha and Buzz to the shore. There was no time for goodbyes because some of the harpies began attacking the Mersprites and the dolphins. They all had to dive beneath the water to escape.

The two friends began running up the beach towards the trees but Buzz tripped and fell just as two howling harpies swooped down at him. The harpies carried a thick net, which they quickly dropped upon the fallen sprite.

Realizing the sprite was no longer beside her, Tiesha looked over her shoulder. Seeing him on the ground trapped in the net brought back images of Talon on the ground trapped in a net with goblins surrounding him. She had almost forgotten him and she suddenly felt doubly guilty for leaving him behind and even managing to have fun with the antics of the diminutive sprite. She managed to push the feeling aside by reminding herself that she had done the only thing she could have in that situation. If she had not, the quest for the Dragon King's help would have been over before it had truly started. Talon had known this, as he had known how difficult it had been for her to leave him behind.

Even though she knew it was not the best course of action, Tiesha began moving towards her trapped friend. If she could get one end of the net away from even one of the harpies, it would give Buzz a chance to escape.

"Run Tiesha," yelled a struggling Buzz as he saw his friend turning back to come to his aid. "I can get free on my own but you must reach the Dragon King. You are almost to his land. Run to the cave among the trees. In it stands the magical doorway I told you about."

Before Tiesha could decide what she should do a harpy holding a long pike landed on the sand in front of her.

"I have you now little human," cackled the gruesome creature. "Grom warned us that the Elfin-faer queen would try sending an emissary to the Dragon King for aid. Your journey is over. The only place you will be going is in my pot to be boiled into a lovely stew. Harhar hehe!"

By this time Tiesha had had quite enough of being chased and seeing her friends trapped by malicious creatures and she did not intend to stand for it any longer. Without a word she dove forward, placing her hands flat on the ground and began swinging her legs up into a handstand. As her legs began to swing upward Tiesha lifted one hand up and reached out to grab hold of the bottom of the Harpy's pike. Letting loose with a loud Karate Kiiia, she torque her body, driving one leg forward and out in a perfect handstand kick, right into the stomach of the harpy.

"Whoosh!" went the harpy as she was knocked right off her feet; the breath knocked out of her as well.

Tiesha came up out of her handstand holding the harpy's pike in her hand. There was no time to feel pride at having executed her kick so well; she had to seize the moment.

Whirling, Tiesha twirled the pike in her hands and lashed out at the harpy that had been diving at her from behind. The harpy had to swerve away to avoid being struck by the whirling pike and losing control of her flight tumbled from the air into a mound of sand.

Holding the pike out in front of her, Tiesha raced back down the beach to where Buzz was still struggling to get out of the net he was entangled in. Yelling loudly Tiesha swung the pike at the two

harpies holding the ends of the net. The harpies dropped the net as they jumped away from the pike swinging at their heads.

That was all Buzz needed. In a flash he was out of the net and blasting away at the two harpies with bolts of sizzling electricity. The harpies now overwhelmed by the pike wielding girl and electricity of the wily sprite had no choice but to beat a hasty retreat up into the air.

Tiesha and Buzz resumed their run up the beach. "If we can make it to the cover of the trees the harpies will not be able to follow us." puffed Buzz as they ran.

Some of the harpies began pelting them from above with some kind of bad fruit that smelled like rotten eggs. But Tiesha had grown pretty adept at dodge ball and Buzz was blessed with amazing speed so they were both able to dodge the fruit as they ran.

As Tiesha dodged a hurtling glob of fruit, a harpy suddenly dove at her from above snatching the pike from her hand. The cackling harpy rode the wind back into the sky, turning in a twisting loop she began another swoop down at Tiesha; who looked up just in time to see the harpy flashing down towards her.

Tiesha zipped to the left then back to the right, ducking under the pike swung by the dive-bombing harpy. As the pike swung over her head Tiesha straightened up and grabbed hold of it, giving it a quick tug and release; redirecting the flying harpy's momentum. The creature lost control of her direction and her wings, tumbling from the sky to crash in a heap onto the sandy beach.

As he ran past, Buzz sent a bolt of electricity into the harpy's rear end. The loathsome creature jumped up with a horrifying screech and holding her injured part jumped back into the air to fly away. Buzz laughed hard.

The two friends had almost made it to the safety of the trees when a large group of harpies dove down from the sky landing in front of them, blocking their route to the trees. Another group landed behind them sealing them in as a third group circled in the air above.

"Ok, who's first?" cried Buzz, a determined expression on his face. Spreading his legs wide the little sprite began charging up his entire body with crackling electricity, waving his hands in the air before him like a cartoon warrior.

"Hahaha. Now it's to the pot with you." giggled one of the foul creatures, showing its pointy fangs. "Tonight we feast like royalty. Yum, yum!"

"You heard him." said Tiesha quietly as she dropped into a loose Karate stance. "Who's first? Weil? We don't have all day you know."

The harpies looked a little worried as they stood there staring at the cornered friends. The two were hopelessly outnumbered and should be easy victims and yet there they stood, so brave and defiant. Not willing to give up in the face of such overwhelming odds. Not only was this unusual for the wicked harpies, whose victims were usually terrified of them, it was also very unnerving. For a moment Tiesha dared to hope that the harpies would just let them go but the moment passed.

Looking to each other for assurance the harpies began advancing towards the cornered pair menacingly.

And at that moment a great roar split the air and big fireballs exploded in the sky like fireworks. The harpies in the air were blown away, tumbling head over heels through the sky.

Those harpies on the ground surrounding Tiesha and Buzz began whimpering and yelping in terror, bolting every which way in an effort to escape what they had seen.

"Harpies be gone! These two are under my protection," rumbled an enormous dragon floating in the sky. His scales shone silver and gold in the sunlight. It was the Dragon King. And the most welcome vision Tiesha and Buzz had ever seen.

The frightened harpies took to the skies, joining their kin who were already flying away as fast as their wings would carry them.

"Phew!" Buzz sighed. Turning to Tiesha he declared. "You know I was not at all scared. Were you?"

"Oh not one bit," said Tiesha with a smile. "But I hope we don't meet those harpies again."

"Hello there, I'm Drago, the Dragon King," boomed the huge dragon, smoke coming from his opened mouth and nostrils. He dropped lower in the sky. "I have been expecting you. Word reached me not long ago of the Goblin's king's allies trying to stop a human child and a sprite traveling to my kingdom. I knew then something was afoot in the southern faraway lands."

"Pleased to meet you," said Tiesha and Buzz together.

"Thank you for saving us from the harpies," added Tiesha.

"You're welcome," said the Dragon King hovering in the air above them. "You might want to close or avert your eyes for a bit." He cautioned. "I'm told that this can be a bit hard on the eyes." Then he began to glow like a small sun.

The glow was so bright that even with her eyes averted Tiesha still had to close them. As the glow began to fade, Tiesha found that she could safely open her eyes. She was amazed to see the Dragon King shrinking in size in direct proportion to the fading glow he was emitting. When he had shrunken down to the size of a horse, he flew all the way down to land on the ground beside the two plucky friends.

"Sorry I could not come to meet you sooner," he began in a rumbling voice that despite its gruffness managed to sound quite melodious to the ear. "But I have been kept busy putting a stop to an invasion of the Ice-Throblin's from The Frozen Highlands at the edge of my kingdom."

"Ice-Throblins are cousins to the goblins," Buzz explained to Tiesha.

"Yes, I believe they timed their invasion with the rampage of Grom, the Goblin King to keep me busy up here so that I could not lend a hand to the good Elfin-faer to the south. They never expected Gossamer to find an emissary to send on her people's behalf. And such an excellent choice I might add. Anyway, you had better be coming with me to the castle." The Dragon King rumbled. "There's a storm coming and you don't want to be out in it."

Uttering just one magical word, the Dragon King transported them all to his castle, which floated in the sky. The sight of such an enormous castle floating serenely among the clouds in the sky was enough to leave even the normally talkative sprite, momentarily speechless. It took him a moment to finally find his voice and when he did; his words came out in a low awed whisper.

"It's magnificent, and very, very big."

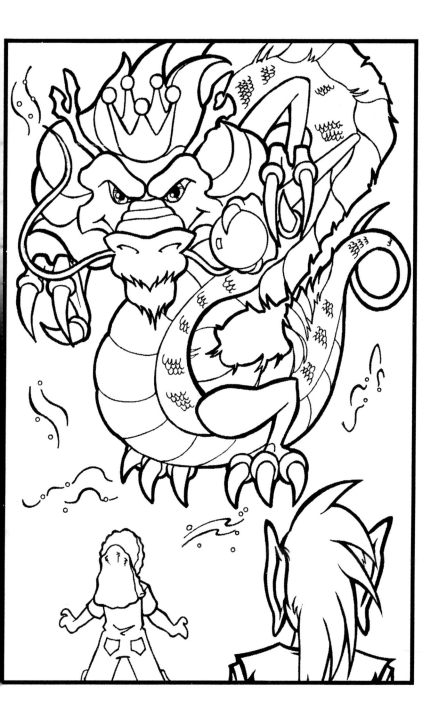

"Yes," said the Dragon King. "It does tend to get that reaction a lot. Say you don't think it's too big do you?"

"I think it should be whatever size you want it," breathe Buzz. "After all you are the Dragon King."

Tiesha found herself in total agreement with her little friend.

With a laugh and a loud welcome the Dragon King ushered them into the castle. The two friends were glad to go indoors as it was very windy and cold this high up in the sky and they were not dressed for this kind of weather.

-CHAPTER ELEVEN-

Gifts for Two

Inside a high ceiling dinner hall he personally served them cherry-berry milk and honey-flower cakes he had baked himself. He joined them in the repast as he explained he could not resist honey-flower cake. As they munched he listened to Tiesha's request for help from the queen of the elfin-faer.

The Dragon King agreed to help readily, stating that he was only too happy to help his friends to the south. And even though he could not leave his land at the present time because of trouble with the Ice-Throblins, he assured Tiesha that he would still help.

"For I can send my help in the form of you two," declared the Dragon King.

On seeing the mystified expressions on both Tiesha's and Buzz's face, the dragon began chuckling in his pleasing rumbling voice.

The Dragon King did not explain his cryptic words only urging the pair to drink as much of the cherry-berry milk and eat as many of the honey-flower cakes as they like.

Despite being puzzled by his remark the two did not need any more urging to drink and eat the tasty milk and cakes as their growling tummies reminded them that they were very hungry. In fact the Dragon King did his best to eat as many of the honey-flower cakes as Buzz. It was a close contest but only because the Dragon King was so much bigger.

After they had finished the meal they went over to sit closer to the fireplace. The Dragon King finally showed them how he intended to send his help.

Summoning a small globe of fire on the tip of a scaly claw he offered it to Tiesha. "Don't be afraid to take it. It is magical in nature and will not burn you. You see this is the help I can offer and it is also my gift to you. Bravery and selflessness such as yours should always be rewarded."

Tiesha held the fireball on the palm of her hand, still a bit surprised but happy it did not burn her. In fact, it tickled as it began to soak into her palm like fiery liquid.

"The magic fire will join with the special quality that you possess and become part of you. You will be able to use it whenever you're in the land of Faraway and in time elsewhere as well. My magic tends to take the form of fires. After all I am a dragon," he laughed cheerfully.

"As the magic becomes part of you, you will be able to use it in many other ways. Those ways will be for you to discover in time. Try to use it wisely and it will always be your light in the dark. And remember, never depend on magic alone, let your wonderful wits and resourcefulness aid you as well and I know that you will have all you need to defeat the Goblin King," the Dragon King smiled.

The Dragon King revealed to them that he still had fond memories of the time when dragons and humans were neighbors and how he missed those times.

"I hope you will return to visit me some day," he told Tiesha with a long wistful sigh. "My gift of magical fire will allow you to return to the Land of Faraway whenever you would like."

"Then you can be sure that I will return to visit as often as I can," smiled Tiesha.

This made the Dragon King so happy that Tiesha was sure that she saw a tear glistening in the corner of one of his great big eyes.

"Ah little sprite," began the Dragon. "Your family has guarded the forests of Faraway for a very long time. In helping Tiesha reach my lands safely, you have not only guarded your forest but all of Faraway as well. Your father would be as proud of you as I am. Well done."

Buzz could hardly believe his ears. He puffed up his chest beaming with pride at the compliment paid him by the great Dragon King himself.

As a reward for his good deeds the Dragon King bestowed a gift of magical wings to Buzz. The plucky sprite was so happy that

he leapt into the air testing out his new wings. Like everything he did the diminutive sprite took to flying like he had been doing it all his life. He put on quite an aerial display for Tiesha and the Dragon King who roared with laughter at the silly antics. After they were finally able to coax the sprite from the air back to the ground Buzz told them that he had always dreamed about having wings.

Only too soon, it was time to go. After exchanging reiuctant goodbyes, for the three had already formed a solid bond of friendship, the Dragon King used his great magic to instantly transport Tiesha and Buzz to the land of the Goblins so that they could rescue Talon the unicorn.

CHAPTER TWELVE

These Frightful Skies

Sneaking up on the goblins was easy because they were all busy jeering at, and taunting the trapped unicorn. Their jeers turned to yelps of fear when a large ball of magical fire suddenly landed right in their midst. One unfortunate goblin was not as quick to scramble out of the way of a larger fellow and ended up being knocked flat on his bum. He landed right on top the fireball. With a loud wail he jumped up and ran off into the bushes, all the while beating at the fire burning the seat of his pant.

As for the other goblins, they had worries of their own as Tiesha threw magical fireball after fireball at them. They were so thoroughly startled that they let go of the net covering Talon scampering every which way to escape what they thought was a rain of fire from the sky. Then Buzz, whooping loudly, swooped down from the sky in a sharp dive, lifting the net off the unicorn, freeing him.

Once freed of his restraints, the unicorn reared up on his hind legs, waving his forelegs in the air majestically. The goblins were now truly terrified and began running away from those flashing hooves with all haste.

In one long spectacular jump Talon landed beside Tiesha. She leapt onto his back as he took to the sky with a quick spring from his muscular legs and a flap of his powerful wings. Together the three friends flew off toward the kingdom of Fief.

The three companions were in good spirits when they stopped for a much-deserved rest. They were exuberant from the successful rescue of Talon from the clutches of the goblins. Buzz was giggling and doing cartwheels on the dry brown grass on top of the little hill they had set down on while Tiesha and Talon watched and laughed at his antics.

They had just sat down to eat when they heard an earsplitting shrieking roar. The sound was so loud that both Tiesha and Buzz clamped hands over their ears.

"What was that?" asked Tiesha removing one hand from an ear that was still ringing.

"Jump on and hold tight we have to make a run for it," shouted Talon, a look of grave concern on his face.

Tiesha was up and on his back in one quick rush, barely able to get a good grip on his long mane before the unicorn took off in a spectacular leap. Buzz was just as fast getting into the air. The air fairly crackled with a discharge of electricity from around his new wings as he used his natural magical electricity to help them generate speed. Already the wily sprite could fly almost as fast as he could run—which was to say, very fast indeed.

"Why are we running away?" asked Tiesha very concerned at the way her two friends were acting.

"It's a griffin," answered Buzz in a very subdue voice. "We have to get away before it spots us."

"Yes," said Talon. "Griffins are very, very dangerous. All the pollution must be forcing them out of their natural habitat. This is a bad development. Very bad indeed!"

The terrible roaring came again but this time it sounded even closer. Tiesha looked back in time to catch a glimpse of a large shadow flitting across a hazy patch of the dark sky behind them. An unexplainable sense of dread filled her at the sight.

Another roar sounded but this time from the dark clouds above them. Tiesha's hair stood on end and a shiver ran down her back at the sound. She did not want to meet the creature that could cause such a reaction just by its roar alone. Ducking her head she leaned in close to Talon's powerful neck, holding tight to his thick mane.

Talon and Buzz both plunged downward in a steep dive before pulling up and entering an especially thick cloud.

Something big and very fast plunged past them down through the cloud. It passed so close that they felt the wind of its passage buffet them, almost knocking them aside.

"Go, go!" Talon hissed to Buzz. "As fast as you can go…

fly!"

Buzz did not need any more urging, he was already away at top speed. He was going so fast that even the powerful unicorn was hard pressed to keep up with him.

As soon as they left the cloud they swerved to the left, plunging into another one. The sound of the horrible roar reached them along with the sound of great wings beating the air.

"We must listen out for a whistling sound," grunted Talon. "It will be our only warning of the griffin descending on us from above. A griffin's favorite hunting tactic is to get above its prey and dive down upon it. Hear that beating of the air?"

"Yes," answered Tiesha. "Is that caused by the griffin's wings?"

"Yes," answered Talon his ears laid back as he listened intently. "The griffin is flying away from us and climbing higher into the sky. Soon it will be too high for us to hear it—griffins can fly higher than any other creature in all of Faraway—then from high up there it will quickly catch up to us and begin a steep dive down at us. Listen for the whistling sound, it will come just before the griffin is upon us and we must be ready."

"Uh oh," exclaimed Buzz, whose hearing it seemed, was even better than Talon's. "Here it comes again!"

"Yes," agreed Talon. "Time to move!"

Talon swerved to the right so suddenly that Tiesha almost fell off his back. It was at that moment that Tiesha heard the whistling sound of a great body plunging down through the clouds towards them.

The whistling sound increased in volume until it was a harsh screech that set her teeth on edge. Dipping a wing to the left Talon dove and changed direction again, this time however Tiesha was ready for it. She even leaned her body to the left to assist the unicorn's sharp turn. Talon and Buzz rode the wind that buffeted them from the griffin's passage.

"Follow me," Talon called to Buzz as he began climbing higher into the sky.

The little sprite did not have to be told twice, he stuck to Talon's side like he was glued there. Talon kept changing directions, diving lower and climbing higher into the sky again and again.

"If I live through this," hissed Buzz. "I will never dare anyone to pull a griffin's tail again."

"Shhhhhh," hissed Talon. "It might hear you."

Buzz was very quiet after that.

The three continued flying as fast as they could, changing direction frequently as they went from one thick cloud to another, taking great care to stay inside the cover the cloud provided. They had traveled a long way before the sound of the griffin faded away behind them.

"I think we lost it," whispered Buzz.

"Yes I think we did," agreed Talon with a sigh of relief.

"But just in case let's remain silent for a bit longer and continue flying as fast as we can," Tiesha told them.

"That is an excellent idea," breathed Buzz. And the little sprite set an example by closing his mouth tightly and leading the way towards the land of Fief.

CHAPTER THIRTEEN

Grom, the Face of Evil

The trio of friends knew there was trouble the moment they entered the Kingdom of Fief. The sky was dark and so thick with roiling black soot that it was extremely hard to see more than two feet in front their noses. Not to mention the soot made breathing difficult for the trio.

"This can't be good," exclaimed Buzz in an unusually subdued voice.

"Hmm," murmured Talon. "The soot blocks out the sun. The magic of the land is waning fast."

"I hope we have arrived in time," whispered Tiesha. She felt a strong sense of foreboding. It was as if all the feelings of dread from every bad dream she had ever had, was now spread through the dark sooty clouds in the sky all about them. She did not like it one bit.

"Do you feel that?" asked Talon suddenly, in a very heavy voice.

"Yes," answered Tiesha and Buzz together, both staring at each other with wide round eyes. "What is it?"

"It's making my hair stand on end, said Buzz with a little shiver.

"It is pure malice," explained the unicorn. "It flows from the Goblin King and is magnified by the presence of his goblin army. The bigger his army the more intense the flow of malice... We must hurry before it fully cripples the land."

"I could go faster if I could see," said Buzz trying, without result, to fan the soot from before his face with his hands. "And this soot is beginning to sting my eyes."

"Hmmm, maybe I…" muttered Tiesha raising one hand from Talon's mane. And with that she called on her gift from the Dragon

King. Summoning the magical dragon- fire she tossed fireball after fireball into the clouds of soot around her.

The effect was immediate and startling. The fire began to burn the clouds, igniting them like large cotton balls. Curiously, the fire leapt from cloud to cloud burning without the slightest sign of heat. What the burning clouds did do however was produce a bright luminous light. The light chased away the darkness and suddenly the three adventuring friends could see as well as if the sun were shining brightly.

"Yeah TIESHA!" whooped Buzz exuberantly. Laughing and flying hoops around her and Talon, the fun loving little sprite was unable to refrain from enjoying the wings he had been granted by the generous Dragon King.

"Well done," smiled Talon to Tiesha. "You are a natural magic wielder."

"You know… I believe my teaching had quite a bit to do with it too," laughed Buzz, flitting around them like a bumblebee.

Tiesha laughed while Talon rolled his eyes at the impish sprite. The unicorn made a wry observation that the sprite had become just a little too adept at aerial maneuvers a little too quickly.

"Hey look!" yelled Buzz pointing downward.

Down below them Gossamer the Elfin-faer queen stood at the head of her people, bravely facing down the invading army of the Goblin King which had finally arrived at the hillock leading directly into the Elfin-faer village. Though the goblins outnumbered the Elfin-faer ten to one and their magic was fading while the Goblin King's continued to grow, the beautiful almost fragile wing folk did not show fear of the big bullies.

A cheer went up when the trio swooped down to land on the hill beside their Elfin-faer friends, joining the line blocking the advance of the Goblin King, his army of goblins and his great machines.

"Get out of my way little folk," shouted the Goblin King, his face one large sneer. "Or I'll run you all over, hahaha!"

"No, we will not allow you to destroy the land of Fief," said the queen in a loud strong voice. "You will turn back from our lands right now or prepare to face the wrath of not only the Elfin-faer but

the Dragon King as well. Turn back now. Do not make me unleash his great power."

"Oh… And where is the great and powerful Dragon? I don't see him. And even if he were here, what would I care," laughed the Goblin King. "Oh he might once have been the strongest of us but my great machines have burned many forests, destroying most of the benign magic of the magical folks, except dark magic. My dark magic just keeps getting stronger. I am now the most powerful in all of Faraway. Your useless Dragon King does not scare me."

"And when there is no longer any trees left to burn in the land of Faraway," he ranted on. "I will then enter the human world and begin my destruction there. And no one can stop me!"

"No," said Tiesha. "You will not pollute Faraway any longer and you will not pollute my world either."

"Oh really? And how will a little girl and an Elfin-faer queen with no magic left, stop me," laughed the king. "Now just stand there while my army crushes you all."

The goblin army began charging forward yelling fearsomely. Laughing in his most mischievous way, Buzz unleashed bolts of electricity into their ranks, making them yelp and scatter. Tiesha hurled magical fireballs at them, receiving more yelps of pain. Not to be outdone, Talon touched his Unihorn to the ground, turning the water on the mucky ground around the goblin's feet to ice, holding them fast.

"Stand fast! You are goblins! We fear no one," yelled the Goblin King at his army. "They are nothing but a few and you are an army." Still hissing in anger at the poor performance of his goblin minions, the king ordered them to charge again.

This time however, Buzz followed Talon's example, sending his electrical charge into the oily ground. Instantly, the electricity spread to the goblins, shocking every one of them standing in the mucky liquid. This was too much for the cowardly goblins they turned tail and fled.

"My cowardly army might have turned tail and run away but I am more than powerful enough to defeat you all on my own." growled Grom.

Buzz flew towards the Goblin King shooting spurts of

electricity at him from his extended fingers. Laughing scornfully, the evil goblin with a simple wave of his hand was able to deflect the bolts of electricity away harmlessly. Another wave and black soot shot down from the polluted sky to engulf the small sprite. Unable to see or breathe Buzz flew right into the side of the Goblin King's machine. Momentarily stunned, the sprite rebounded off the machine to land in the oily muck at Tiesha's feet.

Helping her friend to his feet, Tiesha hurled a fireball at the Goblin King, who simply deflected it away as easily as he had Buzz's electrical bolt.

"Is this how you expect to defeat me, foolish Gossamer?" Grom laughed. "You and your ragtag bunch of misfits don't stand a chance of defeating me. You might as well get use to the fact that I am unbeatable. I am now the most powerful creature in all Faraway. Give up now and maybe, just maybe I will not imprison all of you in stone for eternity."

"Ha, I'll like to see you try," yelled Buzz now back on his feet beside his friends who were all turning their powers on the cackling Goblin King.

"Ok, my pleasure," laughed the Goblin King waving his hand. There was a loud hiss and thick black liquid spurted out from the front end of all his great machines. The gooey liquid began pooling on the ground around the feet of the champions of Fief.

"Oops," yelped Buzz, "me and my big mouth."

"Don't let it harden," yelled Talon trying his best to dance away from the gathering pool.

"Ok." Tiesha began casting the biggest fireballs she could at the dark gooey liquid.

A scowling Buzz threw lightning bolt after lightning bolt into the growing pool while Talon added the magic of his unihorn to the valiant sprite's efforts. Gossamer and her Elfin-faer people also used their failing magic on the dark liquid but sadly all to no avail. None of their magic had any effect on the fast flowing goop. It flowed around them, oozing onto their legs and up their bodies too quickly for them to run away from it. Even Buzz was unable to fly away from it before it had engulfed them completely.

They were all trapped, held fast by the quick hardening goop.

In a moment the goop had finished hardening into dark crystal.

CHAPTER FOURTEEN

Of Courage and Triumph

The Goblin King was so pleased with how he had trapped the champions of Fief that he began driving his great bulldozing machine around and around in a circle, cackling in a bizarre and maniacal fashion. He even sang a tuneless ditty as he drove.

"I'm Grom the king, I'm very mean, destroying lands that are so green, every time I'm on the scene, I do it all in big machines!"

"All is lost," said Gossamer the Elfin-faer queen. "We can not break free. Grom's spell is much too powerful. I am afraid he has won and Faraway will pay the price."

"Hmmm, maybe not," murmured Tiesha as she wiggled one hand until it was free of her crystal bond. "I am new to magic so I have to ask," she continued, making sure to keep her voice low so that the Goblin King could not overhear her. "Can you combine your magic, all at the same time, to form a single spell?"

"Yes we can," answered Gossamer in a voice as low as Tiesha's. "But the Elfin-faer magic is almost all gone. The magic possessed by you, Talon and Buzz is much stronger than all of ours combined."

"My father is fond of saying every little bit helps. The whole is greater than the sum total of its parts." Tiesha told them earnestly as everyone tried their best to lean a bit closer.

"Hey that's a coincidence, my father often said the same thing," Buzz piped up in a whisper. Then looking quite introspective, he continued on in his most serious voice. "You know, I always wondered what he meant."

Despite the gravity of the situation they could not help but smile at Buzz's comment. The mischievous little sprite had the most charming way of relieving the tension of a situation. Tiesha was very glad she had met and made friends with him.

Talon spoke up. "Tiesha's right, all of our magic together will be quite a force to be reckoned with. What did you have in mind my friend?"

Casting a quick glance in the Goblin King's direction, Tiesha's face lit up in a bright sly smile. In a low voice she said. "Ok, now that Grom is so foolishly ignoring us, if Buzz could manage to cut a hole in the bottom of my bag."

"Can I cut a hole? Easy as Sorrel-pie," answered the diminutive electric sprite with a smirk as he sent a sizzling electrical bolt from a finger to her bag.

The bolt burned a long jagged hole in the bottom of the bag that stuck out from the dark crystal holding Tiesha captive. A handful of seeds Tiesha had collected from her travels through Faraway fell out of the hole onto the oily ground at her feet.

A quick whispered explanation of her plan to her companions had them all nodding their heads in agreement that with a little luck and all their magic combined, the plan just might succeed.

Concentrating as hard as they could, they all formed a mental picture of what had to be done and began summoning their magic. Then each one of them directed that magic right into Tiesha. A soft blue glow began to emanate from her body as the magic flowed into her. And then Tiesha reached deep into herself gathering up all of that magic as well as her strength of will, just as Talon had been teaching her to do on the urgent flight back to the kingdom of Fief. When she had gathered every bit of her strength and the magic lent to her, Tiesha summoned up a ball of magical fire with her freed hand.

This ball of fire was quite different from her usual fireballs; for one thing it was not the normal orange red color, it was a blue fireball with electricity crackling all around it. And it was Big, very big—so big that it covered her entire arm, from palm to shoulder.

Then she yelled to the distracted Goblin King. "Oh Grom, the Dragon King sends his regards." Then she dropped the ball of fire upon the seeds floating in the black oily goop on the ground by her feet.

At the sound of Tiesha's voice, the Goblin King looked over in time to see the blue fireball hit the ground. In a flash he spun his great machine back towards the captives he had been ignoring.

"And what do you think you are doing now?" He demanded.

The fireball struck and the seeds were engulfed by it. Then the fireball burst into flames all over the ground, scattering the seeds all over. The seeds soaked up the blue flames and became swollen to ten times their normal size. A musical sound wafted up from the seeds as they began to quiver and shake.

As the Goblin King watched, with a dumbfounded look on his face, thin thread like roots began to sprout from the quivering seeds. The roots thickened, growing longer before suddenly shooting down through the gooey muck seeking the ground below. In the blink of an eye, the seeds burst apart, becoming crawling plants and vines that grew at a tremendous rate.

The Goblin King, sensing something momentous was happening, jumped into action. He cast his mightiest spell and a great roar went up as a bolt of black lightning rushed down from the dark clouds above to strike the sprouting plants and vines.

The black lightning had no effect on the vines, they seem to absorb the terrible lightning and use it to grow even faster.

"Impossible!" growled Grom. "Nothing can withstand the power of my black energy. How could you have done this? You barely had any magic left!"

"Wrong," said Tiesha. "We have each other and together we will always have enough magic left. It is the magic of friendship!"

"And loyalty," added Talon in a strong voice. "Of which you and your kin know nothing of."

"Yes, it is the magic of the heart," said Buzz, not to be outdone. "You would feel it too, if you had a heart."

"The magic of love and nurturing," said Gossamer. "Your greed fuels your need to destroy and fuels the hatred and spite that consumes you. If only you would let go of all that greed and those terrible emotions…"

"I don't need speeches from you bunch of sops," sneered Grom cutting her off. "I like me the way I am. I am still going to trample you, the trees and flowers of your precious lands beneath my great machines."

And with that he began to drive forward, leading the long line of great machines on. The now empty mechanical machines rolled forward ominously, for even without a goblin inside to drive, each one was still animated by the Goblin King's dark magic.

The vines reacted, spreading out at an incredible speed across the goop. Reaching the great machines, the vines began wrapping around them in great leafy coils from top to bottom. A popping sound was heard as the vines began crushing the machines causing the rivets holding the machines together to pop right out of their sockets.

"My machines," wailed Grom as his creations began coming apart all around him. "My beautiful machines. Oh you will pay for that."

Just then the Goblin King became aware of his own predicament as a great vine wrapped itself completely around the great machine he rode in. He was trapped.

"Huh? Nooo!" he screamed.

Before he could do anything however the magically charged vine reached right inside the cabin of the bulldozer machine to grab the squirming goblin in a leafy embrace. In desperation Grom began casting a magical spell. He summoned a bolt of black energy that gathered up a stream of the oily liquid leaking from the wreck of his great machines. The stream of liquid flashed through the air, held by the black energy in the shape of a blade. And striking the vine that held him captive sliced right through it.

He cackled gleefully at his success. "You see. My magic is still more powerful than yours. Ha, ha, ha!"

But just as he was about to crow some more, a second vine pushed its way inside the cabin of his machine and began coiling around his arm. Before Grom could cast a new spell yet another vine had pushed its way inside and began wrapping around his other arm. It was immediately followed by another of the fast growing vines and then another. Each vine continued twining tightly around a part of the evil goblin, becoming ever tighter until all but his head remained free.

"How can this be?" growled Grom as he struggled furiously against the grip of the vines.

"You can't do this to me. I am the Goblin King and you are no more than a mere human child with borrowed magic," he screeched, his face turning red with rage and frustration. "No lowly vine can hold me. I, I will escape. I will…"

At that moment the magical vines began to glow brightly and then the Goblin King's face began to turn a shade of wooden gray.

"What? What is happening to me?" He cried.

"I think you are getting your just dessert," laughed Buzz.

As the Goblin King continued to turn gray and struggle to get free, his magic began to weaken and the dark crystal began turning back to liquid goop, dripping away, freeing Tiesha and her friends.

"I will have my revenge!" The livid Grom roared. "I promise you that all of you will pay for this."

All of the gooey liquid that had formed the hard dark crystal had finally dripped away from Tiesha and her friends, leaving them free to watch the final moments of the wicked Goblin King as he continued to rage at them.

"You think it's over, its not. It's only just begu…" And with that, the final screech to leave the Goblin King's mouth was cut off in mid sentence as his entire body became fully petrified. He had been turned into a living statue of wood.

Tiesha had to smile at the irony in that. The Goblin King had tried to ruin the ecology and in the end had become a part of it. She thought it was very fitting.

"Hey, what do you think he was trying to say at the end?" She asked aloud.

"Nothing important I would bet." laughed Buzz.

"You did it Tiesha," smiled Gossamer giving her a big hug. "You defeated the Goblin King."

"No," said Tiesha. "We defeated the Goblin King. It was a group effort."

"All that matters is that we saved the Land of Faraway." piped up Talon in a very satisfied voice.

"That's right," laughed Buzz, leaping onto Talon's back and off again in his excitement. "We did it."

Whooping in joy, Buzz promptly began creating fireworks in the air with his electrical magic.

The sprite's enthusiasm was so infectious that a few of the Elfin-faer people began a victory dance. Pretty soon Tiesha and everyone else joined in the dance.

"Thank you my friends," cried the Elfin-faer queen flying above their heads. "Now that the Goblin King's machines are gone, all will be well once again in the land of Faraway. Now there is one more task to be done. Will you all, please join me in cleaning up this vile pollution from our lands!"

"I will cast the spell but I will need all your magic for it to work. Just focus your magic collectively as you did against the Goblin King."

Everyone did as the tiny Elfin-faer queen bade, and soon all of their magic flowed to the land—in the form of mystical fire, magical electricity, flower-pollen dust magic and the deep blue unihorn magic—it flowed from each of them. And as the magic flowed, the oily muck covering the ground began to dry up until all of it had disappeared from the hillside.

And at the same time the soot in the sky began to swirl together, gathering into small flakes, then fall from the sky like black snow. As the dark flakes touch the ground they went puff—and disappeared.

Following Gossamer's directions, Tiesha on Talon with Buzz flying beside them soared into the sky and sent magic, fire and electricity into the dark clouds above causing them to burst and spew water in the form of a drenching rain.

The rain did not last for very long but it lasted long enough to soak the ground, washing away the last of the pollutants there. As soon as the rain stopped falling the sun came out, shining down from a clear blue sky filled with puffy white clouds. And a great cheer went up as magical plants and flowers began to poke up from the damp soil.

It had begun—the land was beginning to heal and all would be well again.

"With our magic restored we will be able to help the grass, the flowers and the trees to recover as well as help new ones to grow. It will take time and effort but the Elfin-faer will do all we can to nurture the land as it has always nurtured us." said Gossamer. "Now

it is time to celebrate."

And celebrate they did, holding a big party for all the folk of Faraway. It was the biggest party to be held in the Land of Faraway in almost two hundred years.

After the celebration that lasted two days, Tiesha bid her friends a long sad goodbye before being transported on a rainbow of Elfin-faer magic, back to her room. After she finished materializing from the open book of Faraway stories, Tiesha stood in her room feeling the sense of familiarity seep into her and for a moment she wondered if she had not dreamt it all.

Just then, she felt a curious but pleasant sensation of tingly warmth start in her tummy. In a rush it spread throughout her body. Lifting her arms up and out, she watched a soft sparkling glow start on her open palms before igniting into cool flickering flames that sent shadows dancing along the bedroom walls. The Dragon King's gift!

Then something truly unexpected and wonderful happened. The flame on her hands sang to her, a melodious tune that tickled her insides and set the air around her tinkling in harmony. As the flame-song swelled to a crescendo, Tiesha felt herself rising up, her feet leaving the floor and just like that she was standing on air, floating.

It had not been a dream. A smile dispelled all lingering traces of her sadness. It was real and she could return to see her friends in Faraway whenever she wished! She was happy to be home and she could not wait to write a letter to her friend Shannon, telling her all about her marvelous adventures in the Land of Faraway.

ABOUT THE AUTHOR

K.D. Patrick began writing stories at a very early age, continuing to do so through adolescence and on into adulthood. In addition to the children's book *Tiesha in The Land of Faraway*, he is also the author of *Kyrel's Wugga-wheels Wagon-mobile* and *Kyrel rode Dragons*. He is the author of the comic book series *The Ravager*, the upcoming graphic novels *Lung-mei: the dragon current* and *Code name Wendigo*. The latter titles are penned under his full name Kirk Patrick, to make it easier for readers to identify the author's comic book works and upcoming novels for a more mature reading audience, from his children's book works. An avid martial art practitioner and adept, K.D. Patrick resides in Canada.

You loved reading the exciting story book; now look out for the upcoming graphic novel comic book of "Tiesha in The Land of Faraway".

Coming in 2006 from Alpha Kosmic.

Be sure to join Tiesha in her next exciting magical adventure
with old and new friends in:

TIESHA
BACK TO FARAWAY

EARLY READERS UPCOMING RELEASES!!

KOOL PRESS™

Easy to read - exciting and enchanting

A treat to tantalize the taste buds of those budding readers. These books are especially designed for the early reader, designed with captivating illustrations to engage their imaginations while building invaluable reading skills, featuring authors, subjects and characters children love.

Kyrel's Wugga-wheels Wagon-mobile

Kyrel Rode Dragons

Jeremy's New Bike

Bopsy Bear

Printed in the United States
47190LVS00002B/1-126

9 780973 415209